DEATH OF AN INUA

DEATH OF AN INUA

ARGONAUT

THE INUA HUMPBACK

BOOK THREE

BY

CLIFFORD L. GIONET

Argonaut Humpback Productions

Copyright 2021
by Clifford L. Gionet
All rights reserved

ILLUSTRATIONS BY SUSAN B. SPAIN

PHOTOGRAPHIC EDITING OF ILLUSTRATIONS BY KIM
DAVIDSON

ALL ART IS SEPARATELY COPYRIGHTED BY THE ARTIST
AND INCLUDED IN THE BOOK WITH SPECIFIC PERMISSION
OF THE ARTIST

PRODUCTION ASSISTANCE BY JESS ELLIOTT

Manufactured in the United States of America

ACKNOWLEDGEMENTS

People who live and work in Telegraph Cove provided the inspiration for this book. Captain Jim, Mary, Jackie, staff of Spirit Bear Lodge, wonderful volunteers at the Marine Education Research Society (MERS), and dedicated staff at Orca Lab brought the ideas to life. These individuals and groups are the heart and soul of these pages. This book, *Death of an Inua,* and the two previous books in the series *Angel in Peril* and *Argonaut the Inua Humpback* would not have been written without these remarkable people who live and work on Vancouver Island.

The magnificent humpbacks, orca, dolphins, Spirit Bears, eagles, and other creatures of the marine sanctuary provided the ideas for the three books.

Jess Elliott has become my mentor, friend, and production assistant. Without her, this book and the previous two books in the Argonaut series would not have been published.

The illustrations by Susan Spain are valued additions to the books. Her gift of the graphic presentations to help raise money for the Marine Education Research Society is deeply appreciated.

Photographic assistance with the illustrations, to get them in proper format, was provided by the very talented photographer and photoshop expert Kim Davidson.

My wife, Peggy, has been my partner and greatest supporter for over thirty-five years. Without her, my life would have no meaning.

The topic of organ donation is dear to my heart. My late son, Jason, was a registered organ and tissue donor. After his death in 2009, up to seventy-five people benefited from receipt of his tissue, bones, muscles, and corneas. He lives on in many others.

Dr. Dan Knauf, a longtime friend and cardiac thoracic surgeon gave me the incredible opportunity to witness two organ procurement procedures and a heart transplant. His wisdom and kindness changed my life in a very positive way.

This book, like the first two in this series, is dedicated to my late son Jason for whom Argonaut was named by my dear friends at the Marine Education Research Society. One person writes the words, but it takes many people for the words to become available to readers.

Any errors are the fault of the author.

MARINE EDUCATION RESEARCH SOCIETY

The Argonaut series of fiction novels is written in hope of raising funds for the non-profit group Marine Education Research Society (MERS). This small, dedicated, hardworking, understaffed, and underfunded group of volunteers is trying to save earth from the destructive forces of climate change and pollution. They live and work surrounded by the magnificent creatures of the Vancouver straits in western Canada.

MERS staff are inspiring people who have unlimited energy. They measure their successes in small gains. Their work is vitally important. You can research MERS, Orca Lab, and Spirit Bear Lodge on the web. The scenery of the Vancouver straits area is beyond description. The majesty, beauty, people and animals have left an indelible mark on my life.

All royalties from publication of Argonaut the Inua Humpback series, are being donated to MERS. All contributions will directly support research, education, and marine wildlife response activities.

If you would like to make a contribution, you can follow this link and use PayPal:

Marine Education and Research Society - Donate (mersociety.org)

or send a check to:

Box 1347
Port McNeill, British Columbia
V0N 2R0

TABLE OF CONTENTS

PROLOGUE

In Book One of the Argonaut the Inua Humpback series, we were introduced to Argonaut the Inua Humpback whale. The Inua lives with his pod in the waters near Vancouver Island, British Columbia. Argonaut's Inua powers first became known as he anticipated an attack on the humpback whale calves by a pod of voracious transient orca.

Argonaut is a real whale who spends much of the year in the straits of Vancouver. Argonaut is named after my son, Jason. In Greek legend, Jason is the leader of the Argonauts who search for and find the golden fleece. You can research the story of the real Argonaut the humpback whale on the web.

In these fictional stories, Argonaut, with the help of other whales, and the now friendly orca face off with a group of great white sharks. A truce is negotiated with the great white sharks. For a time, life seems to be fine near the small harbor town of Telegraph Cove, Vancouver Island, British Columbia.

One night, during a terrible storm, a large fishing net breaks loose from a nearby trawler and Raven, Argonaut's son, is trapped. Raven faces certain death. Using his Inua powers, Argonaut reaches out to his human friend, Jason Belliveau, who arranges the rescue of Raven.

In Book Two, Argonaut's mate, Angel, is kidnapped by pirates under the direction of North Korea. The dictatorial foreign power suspects something of the Inua's powers and attempts to capture Angel. With the help of his marine and human friends, Argonaut is able to coordinate saving Angel before she is taken to North Korea.

Jason, Argonaut, Angel, Raven, and many of the familiar characters of books one and two of the series return in this newest adventure. Argonaut's powers are put to the ultimate test.

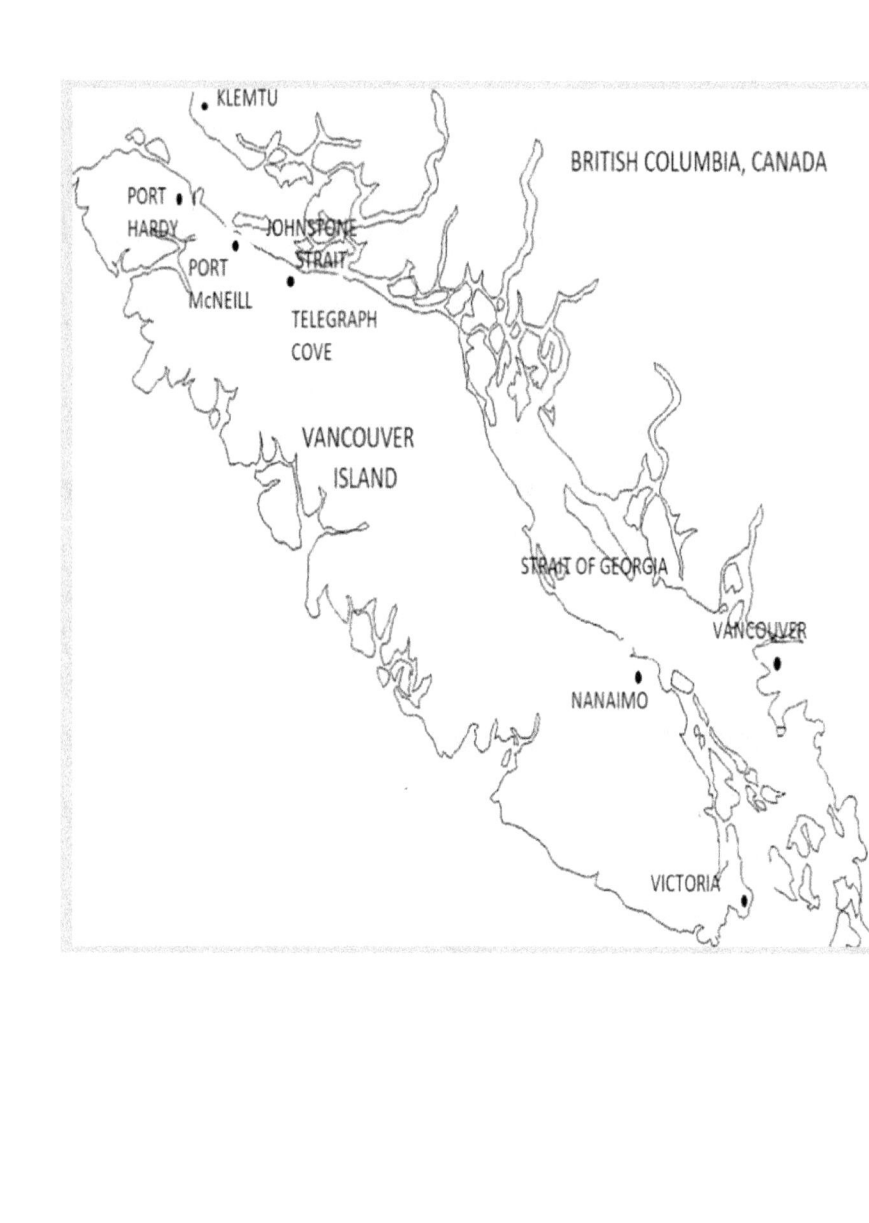

ARGONAUT'S WHALE FAMILY TREE

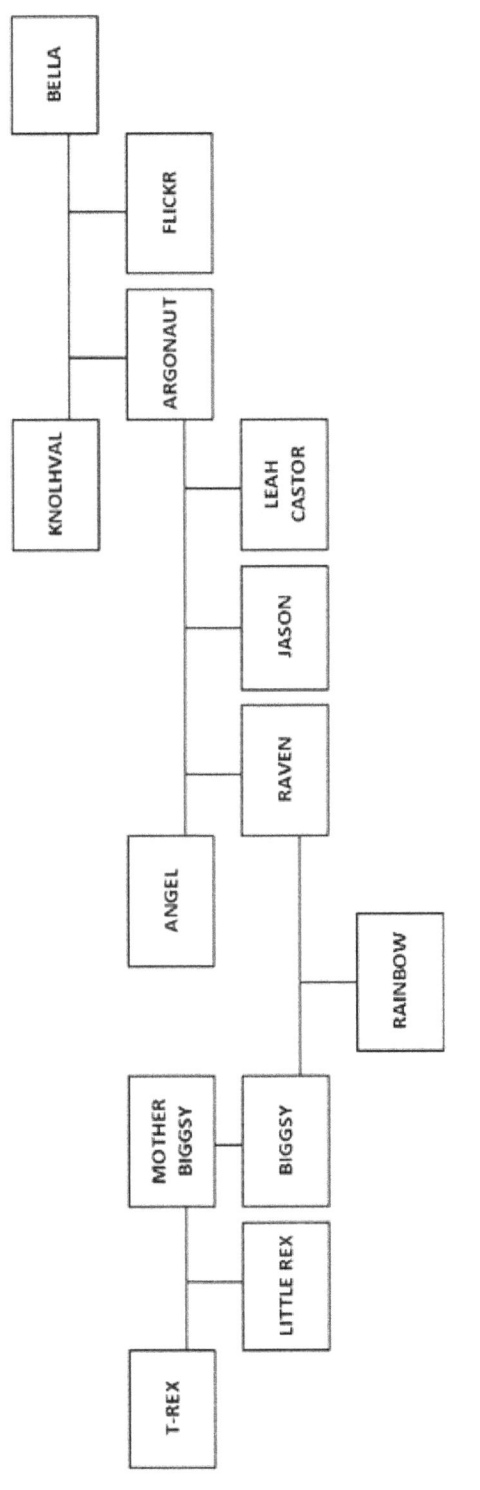

LIST OF CHARACTERS IN ORDER OF APPERANCE

Sitka	Matriarch of Argonaut's pod
Angel	Argonaut's mate
Raven	Son of Argonaut and Angel
Argonaut	Inua humpback whale
Knolhval	Father of Argonaut
Belliveau, Jason	Argonaut's human best friend
Hawk, Matt	Son of Jim and Mary Hawk and Orcella 2 captain
Mendenhall, William (Wild Bill)	Retired Commander of Canadian Coast Guard and current Project HOPE manager
DeFord, Jim	Retired Captain of Canadian Coast Guard and current Project HOPE manager
Pierstorff, Peggy	Lieutenant Commander of Canadian Coast Guard
Bella	Mother of Argonaut (Deceased)
Flickr	Sister of Argonaut (Deceased)
White Feather, Jill	Project HOPE director
Standing Bear, Susan	Project HOPE director
Wildhorse, Jim	Project HOPE director
Redclaw, Joan	Project HOPE director

Raven, Mary	Project HOPE director
Windsong, Charles	Project HOPE director
Fisher, Brigitte	Canadian broadcast and newspaper journalist
Hrafn	First Inua and oldest Inua raven
T-Rex	Mate of Mother Biggsy and father of Little Rex
Guardian	Male humpback whale
Orion	Adopted humpback whale of Argonaut's pod
Hval	Adopted humpback whale of Argonaut's pod
Star	Adopted humpback whale of Argonaut's pod
Biggsy	Raven's mate and daughter of Mother Biggsy
June	Whale taken to ancient burial site (Deceased)
Berryhill, Steve	Project HOPE member
Chief White Feather	Chief of First Nation Kitasoo Xai'xais tribe
Michael	Argonaut's alias
Jason	Son of Argonaut and Angel
Little Rex	Son of T-Rex and Mother Biggsy
Hawk, Jim	Retired Captain of Orcella 2
Patty	Young female humpback whale

Brient, Bruce	Captain/Commander of Canadian Coast Guard
Leibach, John	Chair of University Marine Biology Department
Gionet, LeeAnne	Tutor to Project HOPE directors
Clark, Sarah	Tutor to Project HOPE directors
Choate, Angela	Retired General of US Air Force and crew member on Orcella 2
Kirki	Father of Valent
Namani	Mother of Valent
Valent	Humpback whale that receives prosthesis
Foster, Skip	Marine veterinarian
Mendenhall, Elena	Animal rights activist and real estate agent, daughter of William and Nancy Mendenhall
Mendenhall, Nancy	Orthopedic veterinarian, wife of William Mendenhall
Mendenhall, Marisa	General surgeon, daughter of William and Nancy Mendenhall
DeFord, Terie	Spanish restaurant owner, chef and wife of Jim DeFord
Rothman, L K	UN Secretary General
Mallard, Beth	Marine biologist
Rainbow	Daughter of Raven and Biggsy

Mother Biggsy	Mate of T-Rex and mother of Biggsy
Spirit	Deceased Matriarch of Argonaut's pod
Burns, Ted	Plastic surgeon
Castor	Humpback whale injured in accident
Knauf, Dan	Cardiac thoracic surgeon
Gionet, Marie	Cardiac thoracic surgeon
Peacock, Anne Marie	Cardiac thoracic surgeon (fellow)
McDonnell, Maura	Orthopedic surgeon
Rogers, Bruce	Doctoral student studying humpback whales
Stechmiller, Bruce	Oncology research physician
Lee Pack, Rene	Admiral US Navy
Waters, Steve	Captain US Navy
Leah Castor	Daughter of Argonaut and Angel

LIST OF CHARACTERS IN ALPHABETICAL ORDER

Angel	Argonaut's mate
Argonaut	Inua humpback whale
Bella	Mother of Argonaut (Deceased)
Belliveau, Jason	Argonaut's human best friend
Berryhill, Steve	Project HOPE member
Biggsy	Raven's mate and daughter of Mother Biggsy
Brient, Bruce	Captain/Commander of Canadian Coast Guard
Burns, Ted	Plastic surgeon
Castor	Humpback whale injured in accident
Chief White Feather	Chief of First Nation Kitasoo Xai'xais tribe
Choate, Angela	Retired General of US Air Force and crew member on Orcella 2
Clark, Sarah	Tutor to Project HOPE directors
DeFord, Jim	Retired Captain of Canadian Coast Guard and current Project HOPE manager
DeFord, Terie	Spanish restaurant owner, chef and wife of Jim DeFord

Fisher, Brigitte	Canadian broadcast and newspaper journalist
Flickr	Sister of Argonaut (Deceased)
Foster, Skip	Marine veterinarian
Gionet, LeeAnne	Tutor to Project HOPE directors
Gionet, Marie	Cardiac thoracic surgeon
Guardian	Male humpback whale
Hawk, Jim	Retired Captain of Orcella 2
Hawk, Matt	Son of Jim and Mary Hawk and Orcella 2 captain
Hrafn	First Inua and oldest Inua raven
Hval	Adopted humpback whale of Argonaut's pod
Jason	Son of Argonaut and Angel
June	Whale taken to ancient burial site (Deceased)
Knauf, Dan	Cardiac thoracic surgeon
Knolhval	Father of Argonaut
Leah Castor	Daughter of Argonaut and Angel
Lee Pack, Rene	Admiral US Navy
Leibach, John	Chair of University Marine Biology Department
Little Rex	Son of T-Rex and Mother Biggsy
Mallard, Beth	Marine biologist
McDonnell, Maura	Orthopedic surgeon

Mendenhall, Elena	Animal rights activist and real estate agent, daughter of William and Nancy Mendenhall
Mendenhall, Marisa	General surgeon, daughter of William and Nancy Mendenhall
Mendenhall, Nancy	Orthopedic veterinarian, wife of William Mendenhall
Mendenhall, William (Wild Bill)	Retired Commander of Canadian Coast Guard and current Project HOPE manager
Michael	Argonaut's alias
Mother Biggsy	Mate of T-Rex and mother of Biggsy
Namani	Mother of Valent
Orion	Adopted humpback whale of Argonaut's pod
Patty	Young female humpback whale
Peacock, Anne Marie	Cardiac thoracic surgeon (fellow)
Pierstorff, Peggy	Lieutenant Commander of Canadian Coast Guard
Rainbow	Daughter of Raven and Biggsy
Raven	Son of Argonaut and Angel
Raven, Mary	Project HOPE director
Redclaw, Joan	Project HOPE director
Rogers, Bruce	Doctoral student studying humpback whales

Rothman, L K	UN Secretary General
Sitka	Matriarch of Argonaut's pod
Spirit	Deceased Matriarch of Argonaut's pod
Standing Bear, Susan	Project HOPE director
Star	Adopted humpback whale of Argonaut's pod
Stechmiller, Bruce	Oncology research physician
T-Rex	Mate of Mother Biggsy and father of Little Rex
Valent	Humpback whale that receives prosthesis
Waters, Steve	Captain US Navy
White Feather, Jill	Project HOPE director
Wildhorse, Jim	Project HOPE director
Windsong, Charles	Project HOPE director

ARGONAUT SENSES DANGER

The Sitka pod of humpbacks returned to the straits of Vancouver Island from their winter home near Hawaii in early April 2022. Warming ocean temperatures allowed the pod to return to their marine sanctuary earlier than ever before.

Krill, the main food for humpbacks, were abundant this year. More fish to eat was good for the humpbacks. The whales were famished after not eating for almost six months. The pod quickly returned to its normal routine of feeding during the day and resting at night.

Angel, Raven, and Argonaut took the first night's watch. The three whales circled the pod. Sentries listened carefully for any approaching boats that could prove a danger to their pod. There were no threats from the transient orca pods. The orca had made peace with the humpbacks several years earlier.

Using his Inua powers, Argonaut was able to communicate with all creatures and could sometimes see future events before they occurred.

On this night, Argonaut was unusually quiet.

Angel asked, "What's wrong?"

Argonaut used his mind to answer, "I see a great danger to me in the near future. I am not certain I will survive."

"Are you sure this thing will happen?" Angel asked.

As Argonaut swam next to Angel, he touched her with a pectoral fin. He stroked Angel's back in affection.

"I am certain there is a great danger to me. I cannot see the outcome. It is possible I may not survive."

Argonaut called to his son. He told Raven about the danger he saw in the future.

"Is there anything we can do to protect you, father?" Raven asked.

"We must all live our lives to the best of our abilities. We will enjoy each day as much as we can. I will speak to Sitka and your grandfather, Knolhval. I will explain my concern. I would like to keep this among the five of us for as long as we can. I do not want to worry the remainder of the pod," Argonaut told his son, Raven, and his mate, Angel.

The next morning, Argonaut asked Sitka and Knolhval, his father, to join him away from the pod. Using his telepathy, Argonaut explained to the matriarch and his father, the dark images he foresaw in his future. He explained to the older whales the images were not totally clear in his mind. Argonaut was certain he was in danger. He asked Knolhval to help care for Angel, Raven, and the entire pod, should something happen to him.

His father swam nose to nose with his son. Using his thoughts Knolhval said, "I was gone from our home for many years. I missed much of your life. I will do all I can to protect you, Angel, Raven, and our pod."

"Thank you, father. There is no creature I trust more than you. I will ask Jason, Matt, Commander Mendenhall, Captain DeFord, and Commander Pierstorff to help as much as they can. Raven, Angel, and some of the others in our pod know how to communicate with Jason using his talking machine. I will ask Jason to teach you, in case you need to seek his help."

Knolhval thought back to the time when he lost his mate Bella, to illness, and his daughter Flickr, to a boat strike. He remembered the years of darkness and loneliness in the frozen waters of the Artic. Knolhval's isolation had ended when Argonaut reached out to his father using his telepathic ability. Argonaut asked his father to return to the waters near Vancouver and live with the Sitka pod. It was the best thing that had ever happened to Knolhval.

Since returning to the Vancouver area straits, Knolhval had found peace and happiness. The thought of losing his son was terrifying. He was eager to learn how to communicate with their human friends as soon as possible. If there was an emergency and Argonaut needed help, then Knolhval would not be able to reach Jason or Matt unless he could speak to the humans using the machine. He must learn soon how to talk to the humans using whale sounds the machine could translate to their language.

The three whales rejoined the pod. They tried to act as normal as possible. There was a tension in the pod that many could not identify. Some of the sensitive great whales felt there was grave danger ahead for the pod.

Argonaut had learned to react swiftly and with great effectiveness to any danger. His ability to portend the future was sporadic. Sometimes his visions were clear. Often his glimpses of days yet to come were hazy. The Inua knew his life was in danger. He did not know the final outcome.

PROJECT HOPE

The environmental protection group, Project HOPE, founded by six young Kitasoo of Klemtu was now three years old. Membership in Project HOPE (Help Our Planet Exist) currently exceeded twenty-two million members. Over one-hundred-seventy-six countries were represented by delegates to regional Project HOPE super groups.

The original founding members of Project HOPE were now in their second year of college. Much of the day-to-day operations of the group were managed by former Canadian Coast Guard officers, Wild Bill Mendenhall and Jim DeFord. The student directors met weekly with regional group leaders via ZOOM meetings.

Jill White Feather, Susan Standing Bear, Jim Wildhorse, Joan Redclaw, Mary Raven, and Charles Windsong were back in Klemtu for the summer break from their college curriculums. The young Kitasoo were meeting regularly in the tribe's Big House with Wild Bill Mendenhall and Jim DeFord.

DeFord addressed the group. He mentioned that three major international corporate sponsors had agreed to provide Project HOPE with financial support of one million dollars each per year for five years, with a possibility of future renewal of the grants. The group erupted in cheers. The funds were needed to continue advertising Project HOPE goals and advance their ambitious plans across the globe. Funding political action groups was expensive. The world's population was now in excess of eight-billion people. To make a difference in corporate and political views, more people were needed to exert pressure in the form of voting with their ballots and their consumer purchases. Money mattered when combating large corporations and special interest groups.

Suddenly, Jill slammed the table with her open hand.

"It is not enough," she exclaimed.

"What is not enough?" asked Mary Raven.

Jill looked at her dearest friends and fellow Kitasoo tribe members and said, "We are not enough. We do not have enough members. We do not have enough money. We do not have enough power to effect real change."

Commander Mendenhall calmly replied to Jill's outburst, "We are the largest group of our kind in the world. We have more members and more support than any similar organization. We are getting stronger every day. We cannot stop and just give up. The world is depending on us."

Jill stood and slowly looked at the anxious faces of her friends.

"Ocean levels are rising. Global warming continues unabated. Antarctic ice is melting at unprecedented rates. Population growth is not slowing. We have made no difference. We never will be able to reset the doomsday clock. We are tilting at windmills thinking we can change the world," she told the group with great sadness in her voice. Jill, the most ardent supporter of Project HOPE had tears in her eyes.

Jim DeFord asked Jill, "Do you want to quit the fight and surrender? If we do not help prevent disaster, then who will?"

"We are too late. We are too few. Governmental attitudes, corporate greed, and human indifference will not change quickly enough. We are wasting our time and offering false promises to those that believe in us and Project HOPE," Jill replied.

Susan Standing Bear stood. She waited for the group to settle down. Susan addressed her friends.

"Jill may be right. Perhaps it is too late to stop the world's self-destruction but I am not giving up," Susan stated emphatically.

Charles Windsong, the youngest of the group, rose from his chair. He asked if he could speak. All eyes turned to Charles to hear what he had to say.

With deep sincerity, Charles said, "I have felt this day coming. Like Jill, I too sense almost certain failure of our efforts. I ask each of you the following questions. If not us, then who? If not now, then when? We are the generation that will suffer the most if we are not successful. I choose to stand and fight for what we believe in."

Commander Mendenhall knew there might be one way to effect more rapid worldwide change. His plan involved taking a great risk. He knew he could not make the decision on his own. He asked the group if they could adjourn until the next morning at 10 AM. Mendenhall had a radical idea. He wanted to talk to several people about seeking additional answers to the problems Project HOPE faced.

The group voted to adjourn until the following morning.

As soon as the group left the Big House, Wild Bill called Jason Belliveau.

"Jason, it's Bill. It is urgent I meet with you and our large friend. If I fly to Port Hardy immediately, can you schedule a meeting for this evening for us to talk? I want to bring Jim DeFord along. He needs to know about the big guy."

Jason said he would contact their big friend to arrange a meeting. He agreed to pick up Wild Bill and Jim DeFord at 7 PM from the dock by the Port Hardy airport in his boat, Sadie Princess.

Bill asked Jim DeFord to join him on the short flight to Port Hardy aboard Mendenhall's helicopter.

DeFord agreed to his friend's request. Soon they lifted from Klemtu for the short flight to Port Hardy airfield.

"Why are we going to Port Hardy?" Jim asked his friend and former commander.

"It is too hard to explain. You would not believe me if I told you. It will be better if you see for yourself. It will be worth your time. I should have shared something with you a long time ago. It is important that you to meet a creature that may help us reach the goals of Project HOPE. He may be able to restore the confidence that Jill has lost," Mendenhall replied.

As Mendenhall and DeFord were flying to Port Hardy, Jason reached out to Argonaut with his thoughts. He arranged to meet Argonaut at a small bay about one mile east of the airport. Jason told Argonaut he would be with Commander Wild Bill and Captain DeFord. Jason asked Argonaut to look for the Sadie Princess.

Argonaut agreed. The Inua promised to meet his human friends near Port Hardy. There was potentially great danger to Argonaut and his pod in what Commander Mendenhall was contemplating.

There is a famous quote that says, "Desperate times call for desperate measures."

These were very desperate times for Project HOPE and the world. Therefore, desperate measures were required. If the young Kitasoo abandoned their dreams now there was certainly no other group on earth that could succeed in saving the planet.

ARGONAUT'S SECRET REVEALED

As the Sadie Princess approached the spot where the group was to meet Argonaut, Wild Bill turned to his friend Jim DeFord. Bill explained what DeFord was about to experience would be the most incredible event of his life.

Argonaut rose slowly to the surface near the boat. He used his Inua powers to speak first to Jason and Bill Mendenhall.

"Is your friend ready to hear from me?" he asked.

Jason replied, "There is only one way to find out. Speak to him. Let's see what he thinks."

"Hello, Captain DeFord. My name is Argonaut the Inua Humpback. I am friends with Jason and Commander Mendenhall. They asked me to meet you and share my story."

DeFord turned slowly and looked first at Argonaut, then at Jason. DeFord finally turned back to his best friend Wild Bill. Captain DeFord spoke with wonder and amazement.

"Is this really a humpback that can use telepathy to speak to humans?" DeFord asked.

"Yes, it is really Argonaut the Inua Humpback. Not only can he speak to humans, he can communicate with all living creatures. He is remarkable. I think he may be the answer to Jill's doubts about how Project HOPE can accomplish all the group wants to do," replied Commander Mendenhall.

Argonaut spoke to all three people on the boat. "Let me tell you my story. I first became aware of my Inua powers when my pod was attacked by transient orca. I was able to gather all the humpbacks near the harbor of Telegraph Cove to defend our pod's calves. After the orca attack was repelled, I and my pod made peace with the orca.

"Another time, as great white sharks were starting to enter our sanctuary, I gathered the orca and humpbacks to protect the home we have lived in since time began. After a successful discussion and show of force, the great whites agreed to stay in the ocean. I and my pod repaid the sharks when the great whites were in danger from shark fin hunters. We now have mutual trust and understanding with the great whites.

"When my son, Raven, was trapped in a net, Captain DeFord, you and your crew helped save him. You knew of the danger to Raven because I was able to reach out to Jason using my Inua powers.

"When my mate, Angel, was kidnapped humans helped rescue her. My marine friends the great whites, orca, and dolphins stopped the boats. They enabled you to bring Angel back to me.

"You have been a great friend to me and my pod. I can tell from your thoughts the young Kitasoo, Jill White Feather, has lost faith in her cause. I know Commander Mendenhall thinks if I met Jill and communicated with her that I might be able to help."

DeFord was stunned. Not only could the Inua communicate, but he also had the ability to read minds. DeFord looked at his friend Wild Bill and said, "How long have you known about Argonaut and his amazing abilities?"

"It has been more than two years since I first met with and talked to Argonaut. He has been pivotal in many important events in the Vancouver Island area. We kept his talents a secret for fear of exposing he and his pod to exploitation and harassment. It's time that you and the Project HOPE directors get to know the Inua," Mendenhall explained.

"Can we trust the young Kitasoo to protect me and my pod from exposure to others?" asked Argonaut.

Jason told his Inua friend, "These six young people have worked harder and done more to protect our home and the world from climate change and pollution than anyone else in history. If they promise to keep your secret, they will."

Argonaut told his human friends, "Meet me at the entrance to the harbor near Spirit Bear Lodge tomorrow at the time of the highest sun. Ask Matt to pick up the Kitasoo and bring them to the meeting spot aboard the Orcella 2. I will meet you there. We will explain my Inua powers to these young people. Perhaps my story will inspire Jill and her friends to continue their struggle to save our home."

The following day, at noon, the Orcella 2 anchored near the entrance to the harbor closest to Spirit Bear Lodge. On board were Matt Hawk, Jason Belliveau, Jim DeFord, Wild Bill Mendenhall, and the six young directors of Project HOPE.

Jason asked the Kitasoo if they remembered the trip they had taken aboard the Orcella 2 a few years ago.

"Of course, we remember. It was one of the best weeks of our lives. We had a wonderful time.

That trip was the start of our interest in saving the planet. It now seems so long ago," said Susan Standing Bear.

Jason told the group to prepare themselves for one of the most unbelievable events of their young lives. Just then, Argonaut breached right beside the Orcella 2 and splashed everyone on the boat.

Jason told the group, "Say hello to Argonaut the Inua Humpback."

"Whales can't talk," said Mary Raven.

Argonaut reached out to everyone on the boat and said, "There is more than one way to talk. I am Argonaut the Inua Humpback. I am friends with Jason, Matt, Captain DeFord, and Commander Mendenhall. These waters are my home. I live here with my mate, my sons, and my pod."

The students were speechless. None of them could ever have imagined such a creature existed. Inua were imaginary creatures from ancient stories of the elders. Inua could not really exist here and now in modern times.

"How is it possible that we can hear you?" asked Jill White Feather.

"I can communicate with all creatures. I can read minds, see some events of the future, and affect other creatures with my Inua powers," Argonaut replied.

"Have you always been an Inua?" asked Jim Wildhorse.

"I was not aware of my Inua powers until one day my pod was attacked by orca. I sensed the danger and gathered many whales to defend our young calves from the orca. After the battle I made peace with the orca. I helped protect our waters from a group of great white sharks. The humpbacks made peace with the great whites," Argonaut told the group.

"How did you meet Jason?" asked Jill.

"One day we saw each other underwater. Jason was using an underwater talking machine. We learned to communicate using the machine. Once I became older my Inua powers grew stronger. As I improved my Inua skills we did not need to use the machine to speak to each other. I can read each of your thoughts. I can speak to you using my mind," Argonaut told the group.

Jason explained how the secret of Argonaut had been uncovered by North Korean spy drones. The spies were the ones who kidnapped Angel, Argonaut's mate. He told the six Kitasoo of the revenge attack by the North Korean submarine. Argonaut's secret had been disclosed to only two other people who not here today. One is

Commander Pierstorff and the other is Brigitte Fisher.

Matt told the story of how Argonaut had explained his secret to Fisher hoping she could be trusted to keep his secret. So far, Ms. Fisher had been true to her promise to protect Argonaut.

"Are there other Inua?" Charles Windsong asked Argonaut.

"I once met the oldest Inua that ever lived. He was a raven named Hrafn. He spoke to me just before he flew into the sky for the last time and became a star. There may be other Inua but I have not met them. There are stories among the memory keepers in our pod of ancient Inua, but I have met only Hrafn," Argonaut said.

Argonaut explained to the Project HOPE group that being an Inua was sometimes very difficult. At other times, Inua talents were very rewarding. He told how his powers helped Jason and Matt arrive in time to save Raven from being trapped in a net. He told them of the time he convinced the orca to save the sailors on a boat who survived a crash with a large ferry. It is hard hearing so many thoughts all the time. Like you, I want to do so much to help so many.

"I am only one whale. I do the best I can but sometimes I get discouraged and sad," Argonaut said to the Kitasoo.

Jill looked into the deep dark eyes of Argonaut. She thought she knew exactly how he felt. She knew the Inua understood her frustration.

"Why are we here today?" Jill asked.

"I know of your Project HOPE. I understand you are fighting great odds to save our home and the world. Like me, you sometimes get discouraged, sad, and overwhelmed. I can never give up being an Inua. It is my destiny to help as many creatures as possible. Like me, you have a job that the whole world needs you to finish if we are to survive. What you are doing is much more important and significant than what I can do as just one whale," Argonaut explained.

"We are almost certain to fail. We may not be able to avert global warming, rising seas, pollution, and ever-increasing population growth," said Jill.

Argonaut was quiet for a moment then looked into the minds of each of the Kitasoo and said to them, "You are young, brave, intelligent, and strong of will. There is no one in the world who will try harder to do more than you six. I have faith in you. I see a time in the near future when we will work together. There is danger coming to our waters. I may not survive. My pod, all whales, dolphins, orca, eagles, Spirit Bears, and other creatures of this area need you. Promise me here and now that you will fight for what you believe in. I think the world is starting to listen to your words."

All six Kitasoo agreed to not surrender to the pressure of the tasks they had set for themselves. Argonaut lay on his side and extended his pectoral fin for each of the six Kitasoo to touch. The connection they felt with the mighty Argonaut gave them new strength. They each found a new fervor to fight for Project HOPE.

As Argonaut swam slowly back to his pod, a brilliant rainbow appeared over Klemtu. It was a sign the Kitasoo recognized. Each of the people on the boat was moved by the power of Argonaut's words.

The Orcella 2 slowly made the trip back to Klemtu. Everyone agreed to keep Argonaut's Inua powers a secret. It is important to protect the Inua. Jill sensed Argonaut would become a big part of Project HOPE in the future. She was not sure when or how but he would prove vital to Project HOPE.

THREE INTRUDERS TRY TO
INTIMIDATE THE INUA

The day after his meeting with the Kitasoo and his human friends Argonaut was swimming with the pod near Hanson Island. Suddenly, he looked to the north as he felt danger approaching. The Inua called out to his pod to gather in a group behind him. He asked Raven, Knolhval, T-Rex, and Guardian to gather beside him in front of the pod.

"What is happening, father?" Raven asked.

"There are three humpbacks approaching our area that I do not know. They are large males. I sense their anger and aggression. Stay close to each other and do not act unless I tell you to do so," Argonaut told the members of his pod as they swam by his side.

Soon three large male humpbacks approached the Sitka pod. The three whales tried to swim past the blockade Argonaut had set up as a protective barrier around his pod. The three humpbacks prepared to attack Argonaut as he was the first whale in their way.

"Stop. Who are you? Why are you here?" Argonaut asked as he projected his thoughts into the minds of three aggressive whales.

The three whales were stunned to hear Argonaut's thoughts. They stopped their forward motion. The leader of the intruders replied using his mind.

"We're here to take mates. We heard your pod singing. We want to take three females with us. If you give us three females we will leave in peace," said the leader of the other whales.

"That is never going to happen. We are a family. Our matriarch decides who can become mates. You are not known to us. You will not take any whale from our group. That is my final answer. There will be no negotiations," Argonaut replied.

"Who are you to tell us what to do? You're just an ordinary whale like we are. We have the same right to live here as you do. We will take what we want. If you want a fight then we are ready to do battle. We have come a long way. We are young, strong, and determined to take females from this pod. We will not be denied," said the leader of the aggressive new whales.

"Do you know who I am?" Argonaut asked.

"We don't know and don't care who you are.

You and your pod cannot and will not stop us. We take what we want. We answer to no other creature. Stand aside and let us choose the three mates we want or prepare for a fight to the death," the aggressive whale exclaimed.

"We will not fight you. Also, you will not take any females from our pod. I am Argonaut the Inua. I can read your thoughts. I can see the future. I am powerful beyond your wildest imaginations. I can control many things. Do you know stories of the Inua?" Argonaut asked.

"Inua legends are just fables made up by old whales to pass along from one memory keeper to another. We have never met an Inua. We do not believe they exist. This is your last warning. Move or fight," the leader of the three aggressors said.

Argonaut did not want to harm these three strangers. He and his pod had fought the orca to protect their young. He believed his Inua powers should only be used to help others. He was very reluctant to use his gift as a weapon. Argonaut was thinking of the best way to handle the situation when the three whales suddenly attacked.

With just a thought, Argonaut froze the three whales. Every muscle in each of their bodies was constricted. They could not swim or breathe.

"Listen to me you foolish whales. I am an Inua.

I will die to protect my pod. You are no match for my powers. Even if you want to fight, we outnumber you so you will not win. I alone can easily destroy you if I must. The result of a conflict could be injury or death to many of us. You have no choice but to concede. I will not harm you if you stop trying to attack. Do you understand me?" Argonaut said to the three newcomers.

Argonaut released the three whales from his control. The three interlopers were able to breathe and swim again.

"What are your names?" Argonaut asked.

One whale answered that his name was Orion. Another said his name was Hval. The last whale said his name was Star. Argonaut introduced the three whales to Raven, T-Rex, Knolhval, and Guardian.

"Do you have a pod near here?" Argonaut asked.

Orion, the leader of the three new whales, said they had been forced to leave their own pod. There were too many males in their group. There were not enough females for each male to have a mate. Food was scarce where the whales had been living. Orion and his friends left their pod after being shunned. The three friends had started swimming north towards the brightest star in the sky. They had been on their journey for a very long time. They hoped to find females for mates. The three outcasts thought perhaps they could start their own pod.

"We know we are not strong enough to defeat the Inua. We will leave and continue our journey. There is no place for us here. We are strangers to you. We want to find a home where we can live in peace," said Hval. The three strangers turned to swim away.

Argonaut's father, Knolhval, spoke to his son with his thoughts.

"I was alone for many years in the dark cold waters of the frozen north until you called for me to return here. You and the others accepted me into the Sitka pod. Can we allow these three whales a chance to earn our trust? One day perhaps we may be able to accept them into our pod," said Knolhval.

Argonaut looked first at his father. The Inua then turned to his son. After much thought, Argonaut slowly called out to the three aggressors.

"If you are willing to live by our rules, follow directions given by our matriarch, Sitka, and not force yourselves on members of our pod, we will consider allowing you to stay and live among us. It is a just a trial for now. If you violate our trust, you will be forced to leave. Are we in agreement?" Argonaut asked.

Orion, Hval, and Star all bowed in respect to Argonaut promising to obey Sitka's orders. They would do their best to live in peace in the Johnstone Straight with Argonaut and the others in his pod.

Argonaut took the three new arrivals to meet Sitka. They each bowed in respect to the matriarch. The new arrivals promised to honor everyone in the pod. They would try with all their strength to earn the trust of the Sitka family.

"You did a good thing son. I know what it is like to be without a family. There is enough food for three more whales in our home waters," Knolhval said to Argonaut.

Argonaut looked into the future. The Inua knew that these three whales would be an important part of his future.

As the three new arrivals were introduced to the pod, they each realized this was a family of happy whales. Even though they were strangers and had come with aggressive plans, this pod had agreed to give them a chance to belong to a family. They promised themselves to do their best. The three newcomers desperately wanted to make Sitka, Argonaut, and all members of this pod proud of them.

All creatures deserve a chance at happiness. Argonaut would keep a close eye on the strangers until he was certain they could be trusted. Jason had once told him of a famous human saying. "Trust but verify." The saying seemed appropriate.

PROJECT HOPE FINDS A NEW
SYMBOL FOR THE CAUSE

After meeting with Argonaut, Jason, Matt, and the two Coast Guard officers, Jill White Feather returned to Klemtu. She called a meeting of the executive board of Project HOPE.

"I have a suggestion. I would like your feedback. We are missing a symbol for our cause. We need a graphic image that people can relate to. We want everyone to be able to find a reason to fight climate change, global warming, and all other damaging habits of our current culture. I suggest we adopt the humpback whale as the central image for Project HOPE. The image will be included in all advertising, membership campaigns, on our email headings, and letterhead," Jill explained to the group.

Susan Standing Bear said she had hundreds of pictures of breaching whales from the trip they took several years ago on the Orcella 2. She would select five of the best shots of a whale breaching and present them to the group for a vote on which picture to use.

Charles Windsong asked, "What should we call our new symbol?"

Jim Wildhorse and Joan Redclaw both spoke at the same time and said, "HOPE."

The group agreed it was a great idea to name the whale symbol HOPE. Humpbacks have been hunted by man almost to extinction. Fortunately, the species was saved by cooperation, negotiations, and agreements with countries throughout the world. Saving the humpback whales from extinction proved that humans, if acting in unison, could achieve positive results.

Jim DeFord agreed to contact the large advertising agency that volunteered to help Project HOPE with their publicity campaigns. He would instruct the agency to incorporate the new symbol chosen by the board in all Project HOPE media.

Wild Bill Mendenhall promised to have all Project HOPE email headers modified to include the picture chosen of a breaching humpback selected by the directors.

Humpback whales exist in every ocean of the world. They are magnificent in their size, ability to sing, fish, and migrate. Jill was excited about the idea of a humpback as a powerful visual symbol of

Project HOPE. She was energized to continue the fight for change. Meeting Argonaut and speaking with the Inua had given her and the other directors renewed energy to engage in the many ferocious battles needed to change the world.

Argonaut had been listening to the discussions of the group. The Inua was very pleased that Jill and the other Kitasoo Project HOPE directors decided to use a humpback whale as the symbol for the fight to save the planet. He had a sense of pride that his species was chosen by Project HOPE directors to represent their cause.

The Inua reached out to the executive board. He congratulated and thanked them on their decision to use a whale as the new symbol for Project HOPE.

"I have great expectations for your group. There will come a time, in the near future, when we will work together to advance the efforts you are pursuing. You make me proud to be your friend," Argonaut said to the Kitasoo.

"How can we work together if we must keep your Inua powers a secret?" Jill asked.

"As I look into the future, I see a day when my voice and maybe even my identity may need to be revealed to the world. If and when that happens, perhaps we can speak as one voice for the changes needed to save earth. Whatever the future may bring, never give up your dreams for a better world. My kind was saved by people just like you working to protect us," Argonaut said.

"Meeting you has changed us forever. Knowing that even one Inua exists and that animals have such incredible intellect gives us more drive to succeed," Susan told Argonaut.

"Until the time is right, we must protect my pod from harm by not disclosing my Inua power. I am trusting you with my life and the lives of all of those in my family. I know you will not disappoint me," said Argonaut.

Each of the young Kitasoo was lost in their own private thoughts. They were pondering the significance of what they had learned about this one incredible humpback whale.

The directors reached out to their regional officers with a memo explaining the new humpback whale symbol. They had chosen one of Susan's pictures of the breaching T-Rex as the new core image for Project HOPE.

Soon chapters were running fundraising campaigns by selling humpback t-shirts, humpback memo cards, and copies of the T-Rex photo.

The image was spreading across the world. Everyone knew humpies, at one point, had been close to extinction. Human actions had saved the humpback whale species. If humans could save one species, perhaps a worldwide coordinated effort could accomplish even more.

PROJECT HOPE

"**H**elp **O**ur **P**lanet **E**xist"

KLEMTU ISLAND

BRITISH COLUMBIA, CANADA

New fax coversheet and brochure cover for Project HOPE mailings and emails.

THE POD GOES TO SCHOOL

Argonaut and Jason met near Hanson Island early one morning.

"How are you, my Inua friend?" Jason asked.

"So far, so good. I am worried. If something happens to me, my pod might not be able to communicate with you and other humans. Are you willing to teach the other members of my pod to communicate using your underwater machine? You can use the same method you did with me when we first met. There are now thirty-one whales in the Sitka pod," Argonaut explained.

"I still have the Wet PC Underwater computer and the flashcards we used to establish your vocabulary. Why don't we start by teaching a group of five whales? If we are successful, we can teach the entire pod. Does that sound like a good idea to you?" Jason asked.

Argonaut called for Knolhval, Raven, Angel, Sitka, and T-Rex. As they gathered around the Inua he explained Jason was going to use his computer to help him learn each individual whale's voice.

Argonaut explained the need for each whale to be able to communicate with Jason in case there was danger. Argonaut said that the pod needed to be prepared, in case he was not always there to help.

Raven asked his father, "What could happen to you father? You are an Inua."

"I am just a whale. I'm not immortal. I can be hunted, killed, trapped in a net, struck by a boat or get sick. If the entire pod learns how to speak to Jason using his computer then we will be safer. Once the five of you have mastered speaking and listening to sounds using the machine, we will teach the others in the pod to do the same. Humans can do many things we cannot. They saved you when you were trapped in the net. They helped save your mother when she was kidnapped. They can use boats and machines that fly in the air. They had medicine for Biggsy when she was sick," Argonaut told his son.

Raven gave some thought to his father's words. He agreed it was important for the pod to be able to communicate with Jason and other humans.

The work with the first five humpbacks went quickly. All words Argonaut had learned were stored on the computer's hard drive. The other whales easily understood the sounds Argonaut made. The computer was able to correctly interpret virtually all the sounds each individual whale made. With a little practice the whales mastered talking to Jason using the wet PC.

Argonaut asked Jason to record a new sound for all the whales to use. It was the sound for danger. Argonaut made the sound whales use to warn each other of danger. Jason added the new sound to the vocabulary stored in the memory of the Wet PC. It was like a human calling 911. If Jason heard that sound, he knew the pod needed help immediately.

Within a week all members of Sitka's pod had experience interfacing with the computer. They could recognize words expressed as whale sounds by the machine. The computer could also interpret each expression made by each individual whale of the pod.

Jason suggested they also teach Matt Hawk how to use the Wet PC. The program, software, and voice recording data were copied and transferred to Matt's laptop. Using the hydrophone on the Orcella 2 Matt could communicate with the whales if Jason was unavailable.

Argonaut sensed that soon one of the humans would need to reach out to the whales for help. He felt more comfortable now that Matt, Jason, and the entire pod could communicate with each other using the Wet PC computer and vocabulary program.

After the last training session using the computer, Angel approached Argonaut. Using her thoughts, she asked him what danger he saw in the future.

"You know me too well," Argonaut said to his mate.

"We have been partners, friends, and mates for many years. You helped save my life. We have a family together. I sense fear and darkness in your thoughts," Angel said to her Inua mate.

"I am not certain of the exact details. I do see flashes of a horrible accident that hurts a whale, not of our pod. I also see pain and perhaps death in my own future. These two events are somehow related. This is why I wanted all the whales to knew how to talk to Jason and Matt. I am not afraid to die, because to live in fear of death is to rob us of the joy of living each day the best we can," said the Inua.

"I want us to grow old together and spend many years by each other's side. Together we are more than either of us separately. You have done so much for so many creatures. I cannot imagine my life if you were not with us," Angel said.

Argonaut swam to his mate. He touched his nose to hers.

"I promise to do everything I can to be with you as long as fate allows. We have many friends. We have two strong and healthy sons. We have a wonderful home. My insights of the future are not always clear. Perhaps I am wrong in my vision. Whatever happens, I will fight with all my power to be with you," the Inua explained to his mate.

RAVEN AND T-REX TO THE RESCUE

A few days after the pod finished their communications training with the Wet PC, Matt had the program and data transferred to his laptop. He could practice listening to the whales and translating their calls into English.

On a clear spring evening Matt was aboard the Orcella 2, anchored a few miles west of the northern entrance to the straits near Vancouver Island. He was currently working on a project for the Canadian Broadcasting Company. He was hired to make a documentary on the best views of nature in Western Canada. On this night, he was photographing star trails.

A star trail is a slow-motion photograph that allows the viewer to see the effects of the rotating earth. When done correctly, the photograph shows many swirls of light. The earth rotates and the stars are stationary. The motion leaves a trail of light in the picture from every visible star. It looks as if the stars are moving, leaving a trail of light in their wake.

Matt is a very accomplished photographer and documentary film maker. He was using the new mirrorless Canon EOS R5 camera. He set the shutter speed at ninety seconds. The camera had a short lens, focused to infinity, set with the widest opening possible. The autofocus feature of the camera was turned off. To make the shot work on a moving boat in the Pacific Ocean, Matt was using a multiple gyroscope and gimbal stabilization system. The camera stabilizing mechanism was invented for military defense systems in the late twentieth century.

The best shots of star trails need to be taken far away from all ambient light. For this reason, Matt was anchored two miles out to sea. Matt turned off all the running lights aboard the Orcella 2 to further reduce light interfering with his star trail photographs. There was no moon, the sea was calm. The conditions gave Matt the perfect opportunity for taking star trail pictures.

After three hours of shooting the stars Matt pulled up the anchor. He tried to start the engine. There was no response as he turned the key. The starter would not engage. None of the lights would operate.

The likely cause of the problem was a faulty alternator. Just like in a car, a bad alternator can cause the battery to drain. A dead battery means you cannot start the engine.

Matt went down to the engine compartment carrying a flashlight. He checked the connection of the battery cables to the three marine batteries. Everything seemed to be in its proper place. As he was bending over to check the alternator, he dropped his phone into the bilge. It sank in about ten inches of salt water. It took him several minutes to locate and retrieve his phone. After being in the salt water for so long his phone did not work.

Matt was an experienced sailor, so he did not panic. Even though all onboard electronics and his phone were no longer operational, he did have a handheld emergency locator beacon. He could activate the beacon to notify the Coast Guard of his need to be rescued. Matt activated the beacon. He was prepared to light emergency flares once he heard the rotors of a rescue helicopter or heard the engines of a Coast Guard ship approaching his location. Matt expected to activate the flares within thirty minutes. He was only a few miles from the Port Hardy Coast Guard Station.

What Matt did not know was four days ago, there had been a very large series of solar flares that were now affecting most electrical systems and electronic devices in the northern hemisphere.

Matt's emergency signal was not received by the Coast Guard.

After waiting more than two hours with no response to his emergency beacon signal Matt began to worry. He knew by using star navigation that he had drifted further west into the Pacific away from Vancouver Island. The Orcella 2 was getting closer to international shipping lanes. Large tankers carrying oil and natural gas from Alaska to the United States use these lanes with great frequency. At just sixty feet in length, the Orcella 2 would be nearly invisible to a large tanker traveling to or from Alaska. Modern day tankers can exceed twelve-hundred feet in length. These floating behemoths are difficult to turn or stop quickly. Matt needed to be rescued soon to avoid danger.

Matt remembered he had the underwater whale sound software on his computer. He connected two small underwater speakers, via USB ports, to his laptop. His laptop was powered by an internal battery so even without power from the boat batteries his laptop operated. He lowered the speakers over the side of the boat. He typed on his laptop keyboard a message that was instantly translated into whales sounds. He wrote, "Matt needs help. Boat broken. I am three miles west of north Vancouver Island. Answer if you hear this."

Raven and T-Rex were located far north of the rest of the pod. They were searching for new food sources for the ever-increasing number of whales in the pod. Both whales heard Matt's call for help.

Raven reached out using his thoughts for Argonaut.

"Father, did you hear Matt's call for help?"

Argonaut replied that he had in fact heard Matt's call. Argonaut used his telepathy to contact Jason.

The Inua asked his friend to contact the Coast Guard and ask that help be sent to Matt as soon as possible.

Jason responded to Argonaut that all radios were currently not working. Jason had no way to reach the Coast Guard. Commander Pierstorff was on vacation in France. There were no other humans in the Coast Guard that Argonaut could reach by telepathy, without risk of exposing his secret Inua identity.

Raven and T-Rex asked Argonaut if they should try to rescue Matt.

The Inua told his son and T-Rex to find Matt and do what they could. Jason was driving from

Nanaimo to Port Hardy to alert the Coast Guard. He was at least two hours away.

As Raven and T-Rex swam towards Matt's location they called out using whale sounds. Matt heard their calls and was able to use the Wet PC program to translate their voices.

"We are coming to help. Do not worry," the whales said.

As his son and friend were swimming towards the Orcella 2, Argonaut used his powers to reach into Matt's thoughts. The Inua explained the radios were not working. He told Matt that Jason was driving to the Coast Guard station in Port Hardy to seek help.

"Find two large ropes to put around Raven and T-Rex. They will pull the Orcella 2 closer to land. We know the ropes work because we pulled June's body to the sacred burial grounds after she died. Raven and T-Rex will be there soon," Argonaut told Matt.

Matt tied large loops in two one-hundred-fifty-foot ropes. He tied one rope to a cleat on the port side of the boat. The second rope was secured to a cleat on the starboard side. He was ready for Raven and T-Rex.

Within thirty minutes the two large humpbacks arrived. Matt put one loop around Raven. The second rope was looped over T-Rex. Slowly the whales put tension on the lines. The two humpbacks used their massive flukes to start pulling the Orcella 2 towards Vancouver Island. Fortunately, there was a stiff wind from the west. The tide was coming in. It was a slow process, but with each flip of their flukes Raven and T-Rex pulled the Orcella 2 closer to their home waters.

Jason reached the Coast Guard Station and told them of Matt's emergency. The station commander said none of the electronic devices were functioning. The commander informed Jason it was not safe to send a rescue boat or helicopter after Matt since navigational devices were not operational.

While Jason was on his way to the Coast Guard Station, Argonaut asked Orion, Hval, and Star to swim with him as fast as they could to help Raven and T-Rex pull Matt's boat to safety. Argonaut wanted to help his son and old friend pull Matt and the Orcella 2 to safety. The three newest pod members would be tested. Argonaut would soon learn if they were willing to be part of the pod, when there was work to do.

The four whales swam as fast as they could north then west into the Pacific Ocean from the Vancouver straits. Soon they heard the calls of

Raven and T-Rex. Argonaut asked Star and Orion to replace Raven and T-Rex in the loops. With Matt's help, the two whales were fitted with the loops and they started to swim following Argonaut's instructions. Raven and T-Rex were exhausted.

After about two hours, Argonaut and Hval relieved Star and Orion. They began working as a team pulling the Orcella 2 closer to Port Hardy.

Jason left Port Hardy aboard the Sadie Princess. He was making his way as fast as possible towards Matt. Jason did not need navigational aids as he could communicate directly with Argonaut and receive directions from the Inua to the location of the Orcella 2. Finally, Jason saw the six whales and his friend's boat.

Matt, untied the loops from Argonaut and Hval. He tossed the ropes to Jason who then tied them off on cleats aboard the Sadie Princess.

Jason's boat started pulling the Orcella 2 towards Port Hardy. It was nearly dawn as the two boats approached the docks at Port Hardy.

Matt reached out to Argonaut and thanked him and his pod for saving his life.

The Inua said, "You and Jason saved my son when he was caught in the net. I owe you his life. You have my lifelong promise of friendship. We are all glad we could help."

The six whales swam quietly into the dark waters back to their pod.

Argonaut thanked his son and T-Rex. He then reached out to the three newest pod members. He thanked them each individually. He told them the story of Raven being caught in the net and how Matt and Jason had saved his son's life.

"Today, you have shown that you are trustworthy, hardworking, and loyal. Someday my friends, you may be needed to save me or others in our pod. You did well. I will be at your side if you ever need my help," said the Inua.

Orion, Star, and Hval knew something important had happened this day. For the first time in their lives, they felt as if they had found a home among friends. They were proud. They were part of a family that cared for and respected them.

HOPE AND THE LONGEST DAY

An online virtual meeting of regional Project HOPE leaders was held on May 1, 2022. There was renewed enthusiasm among the leaders and their chapter members after the breaching humpback symbol for Project HOPE was publicized.

Membership numbers, corporate sponsorship, and governmental support across the world were all growing rapidly. In the international online forum, Jill asked the members if anyone had any ideas for a worldwide event to capture the attention of those people who were not yet members or supporters of Project HOPE.

Steve Berryhill, a representative from Ireland, who ran an advertising agency in Dublin, suggested a worldwide Project HOPE Day to be set each year on the day of the summer solstice. In 2022, the longest day of the year would be June 21. There was widespread agreement among the national representatives in support of this idea. A policy group of twenty regional representatives was appointed to outline events that would highlight the activities of the first Project HOPE Day.

Suggestions included marches; voter registration drives; letter writing and email campaigns to remind legislators of the need to act on climate change and pollution issues; and membership ad campaigns to run in newspapers, on television and radio stations and much more.

Jill reminded everyone there was only six weeks to prepare for HOPE Day. She asked all chapters and their members to start planning activities for their cities and countries.

In Canada, the Project HOPE directors contacted Premier Guyaen. The young Kitasoo asked for permission to address the Canadian Parliament at the legislative headquarters on Parliament Hill in Ottawa. Guyaen agreed to ask the heads of the Canadian Senate and the House of Commons for permission for six Kitasoo to address a joint meeting of the parliament on June 21. The legislative leaders agreed to convene a joint session in honor of International Project HOPE Day.

Similar actions were taken in democracies around the world with great success. Apparently, the number of Project HOPE members exerting pressure was sufficient to garner attention from legislators in almost every country.

Each regional and local chapter had a different action plan. Under general guidance from the Kitasoo directors, chapter members began making signs, writing letters, asking for free advertising time in the electronic media and in the press. All social media sites began distributing messages submitted from users about International Project HOPE Day. City chapters were allowed to design a campaign best fitted to their locality.

The summer solstice carries a great significance in many cultures. Not only is it the longest day of the year, it is the beginning of summer north of the equator. Nature's beauty is at its peak in the warmth and sunshine of summer in the northern hemisphere. In the southern hemisphere, the winter solstice is on the same day as the summer solstice in the northern hemisphere.

The themes for both the northern and southern hemispheres were different. However, the central message of harmful climate change, dangers of pollution, and species extinction were the same.

As the first International Project HOPE day approached, the directors were busy coordinating events on a worldwide level. Commander Mendenhall and Captain DeFord arranged the travel plans for the Project HOPE leaders to fly to

Ottawa. The address to the Canadian Legislature would be carried live on Canadian Broadcasting Corporation media outlets.

CISCO, the large software company, offered to make the HOPE address to the Canadian Legislature available free of charge as a video conference using its newest WEBEX software. Similar offers were made to speakers at other meeting sites all over the world. CISCO hoped to set the world record for most simultaneous attendees at the many different video conferences. This world record would be a great marketing tool for WEBEX.

The six Project HOPE directors each wrote their own speech. Conservation of resources; global warming; pollution of the air, land and water; alternative energy sources and species extinction were the main topics. Each director planned to address a single topic. Each speaker was granted up to five minutes to address the Canadian legislative leaders.

Argonaut frequently listened to the thoughts and communications involving Project HOPE. He explained what was happening to his pod.

Knolhval asked his son if these young people could really save the world from self-destruction.

"I do not know father. I cannot see that far into the future. I know these are smart young people are doing everything they can to help. I think there will be a time in the near future when I may work with them to help convince all people of the world to work together for change," Argonaut told his father.

"How can you help without the world discovering your Inua powers?" Knolhval asked.

"It may be necessary for an Inua to speak to the world. I will try to keep my identity a secret. The reason I now wear the cover on my fluke is to hide the A on my tail from people who may want to harm us as they did Angel," Argonaut said.

As father and son swam in unison back to the pod, they both had fears about the future. Argonaut knew there was great danger coming to the straits.

JASON AND THE SEA LION

While on routine patrol as part of his Coast Guard Auxiliary volunteer assignment, Jason spotted a sea lion floating near the surface of the strait wrapped in what appeared to be a large rope. The sea lion was having trouble staying afloat because of the drag of the long rope. It was obvious the animal was in distress. Jason was in water too deep to anchor the Sadie Princess so he could not secure his boat, then swim to the animal to cut the rope from the sea lion. Every time he tried to get close to the animal with his boat, the animal got scared and swam away.

Jason needed help quickly before the sea lion drowned. The animal was weakening from trying to stay afloat while carrying the weight of the heavy rope. There were no other boats near the northern end of the Johnstone Strait. He called out for Argonaut. Jason explained the problem. He asked Argonaut if there was a way to get help for the sea lion.

Argonaut told Jason he knew exactly the right

creature to cut the rope from the struggling sea lion.

Argonaut reached out to his friends the great white sharks who were living outside the northern harbor of Vancouver Island. Argonaut had made peace with the great whites several years ago. With help from Raven and Guardian, Argonaut had saved a young great white from being killed by shark hunters. Argonaut had driven the shark hunters from the Vancouver area. The great whites promised to help Argonaut, if ever asked.

"Great whites, can you hear me?" Argonaut said as his thoughts reached out to the sharks.

"Hello, Inua. How are you and your pod?"

"We are all fine. I need a big favor, if you are willing," Argonaut said.

"We promised to help you after we made peace. Since you and your friends saved my son from certain death, we are in your debt. How can we help?" the senior great white asked.

"Near you, one of my human friends is trying to save a sea lion from drowning, after the animal was caught in a large rope. I cannot cut the rope since I have no teeth. You and your family have the largest teeth in the ocean. It would be easy for you to cut the rope. Are you willing to try and save the sea lion from drowning?" asked the Inua.

There was a long pause of silence. The great whites had promised to help the humpbacks but had made no promise to help sea lions.

"The sea lion is food for us. We would need to enter your sanctuary which we said we would not do, if we were to be left in peace," the shark finally replied.

"I know it is a great challenge for your kind to help a sea lion. The animal is in the sanctuary that you promised not to enter. If you help this creature by cutting the rope you will repay me and my pod for saving your son from the hunters. I would not ask this of you if I did not trust and respect you. One day, you may need me again. Remember, I and my human friends drove the shark hunters from these waters. Because of my pod and the humans, you now live in peace and safety. Please, do this for me," Argonaut said.

"It will be done as you wish. Tell your human friend I will be there as quickly as I can. Also, use your Inua powers to tell the sea lion not to be afraid of me. I will not harm him. I will cut the ropes. He will be free. The sea lion must be very still when I approach so I do not harm him," said the large shark.

As the great white started swimming towards the Sadie Princess, Argonaut told Jason what was going to happen. He also spoke to the sea lion. Argonaut told the frightened and exhausted sea lion not to be afraid of the shark. No harm would be done to the sea lion. He had the promise of Argonaut the Inua.

The sea lion knew stories of the powerful Inua. He calmed himself as he struggled to stay afloat. Within minutes the twelve-foot shark appeared next to the struggling sea lion. The shark gently grabbed and cut through the rope using his teeth. The rope sank and the sea lion was saved. Jason recorded a video of the rescue. It was unlike any other moment in animal history. The largest predator in the ocean was seen saving a helpless food source.

Jason watched the shark disappear into the depths as the sea lion swam east to the rocks near Telegraph Cove where his colony lived.

The sea lion reached out to Argonaut with his mind. He said "Inua, can you hear me?"

"I can hear you, little friend," Argonaut replied.

"I owe you my life. Only you could make a shark save me," the sea lion told Argonaut.

"I did not make the shark save you. He acted out of friendship to me and the other creatures of the sanctuary. Different creatures can be friends. Perhaps, one day the sharks may need you as a friend," Argonaut told the sea lion.

"We are natural enemies with the sharks. We are food to them. However, if you ever ask me to help a shark, I will do all I can to repay the kindness," the sea lion said.

Argonaut thanked the shark and reminded him of the peace between the whales and sharks.

"We are in your debt great shark. I know it was hard not to kill the helpless sea lion. You are an honorable and trustworthy animal," said Argonaut.

"I do not plan to ever save another sea lion. It took all my will power to avoid eating him. I think that was one lucky sea lion. Be well my friend," said the great white as he rejoined his family in the cold depths of the ocean near northern Vancouver Island.

Jason reached out to Argonaut and said, "That was one of the most incredible sights I have ever witnessed. A great white shark saving a sea lion at the request of an Inua humpback. You never cease to amaze me, my Inua friend."

Argonaut smiled and rejoined his pod who were swimming near the sea lion rocks just outside of Telegraph Cove. Argonaut had never given much thought to the sea lions who lived in these waters. They were not food to the humpbacks. The sea lions posed no danger to the humpbacks. Argonaut began to understand what the Kitasoo Project HOPE directors were trying to do. They wanted to save all creatures, not just their own kind.

The whole of Argonaut's world consisted of the straits near Vancouver Island and his winter home near Hawaii. Like many humans, he was concerned with his small section of earth. Project HOPE was trying to save all creatures wherever they lived.

Even a great Inua like Argonaut has much to learn from others like the young Kitasoo.

SEA LION CAUGHT IN ROPE

NEW HOME AND NEW DIRECTORS FOR PROJECT HOPE

The six original Project HOPE directors, who all had recently turned twenty years of age, along with their two executive directors, Commander Wild Bill Mendenhall and Captain Jim DeFord, shared a very cramped work space. Their area consisted of two small adjacent cabins on Klemtu. It was difficult to move in the crowded environment. The workflow was inefficient. Captain DeFord, at the May directors meeting, suggested building a new six-thousand square foot building to house all Project HOPE equipment and offices.

The directors asked what the new building would cost. Captain DeFord said based on preliminary estimates, the total cost would be about one-and-one-half-million dollars.

"How can we afford such a huge expense? Our budget for the 2022 fiscal year has been set and all our funds are committed," said Jill White Feather.

"It will not cost us a penny. Premier Guyaen has offered to pay for the building with funds from the capital outlay budget of the Canadian Developmental Building Fund. He wants to use as much local labor and materials as possible to help stimulate the local economy. Project HOPE has brought much good publicity to Canada. You are internationally renowned celebrities. The building shows Canada is dedicated to helping control climate change and reduce pollution. This is also a national election year. Your work has brought much favorable attention to the many legislators who support your efforts. It is estimated that it will take twelve months to complete the building. Chief White Feather has agreed to lease the land for the building to Project HOPE for ninety-nine years at one-dollar per year. If the directors approve, we can search for architects and builders," DeFord explained.

After a unanimous vote of approval, DeFord and Mendenhall promised to present ideas and concepts for the building at the next regular directors meeting.

The next order of business was an item suggested by Wild Bill Mendenhall. "Our group is expanding rapidly throughout the world. You are consumed with managing many different issues.

Klemtu is remote, even with our improved electronic capabilities, communication and travel are challenging. I would like to suggest a change in the group structure. Each member country would elect a seven-member board of directors. Directors would serve a two-year term, with a maximum of two consecutive terms. From each national board one member would be selected to represent the country in a continental assembly. The assembly for each continent would meet once a year in a different location. Initially, you would retain your status as executive directors and be a part of the North American Continental Assembly. We also need to provide a succession plan. There will come a day when one or more of you move on to different lives and careers. You may not have as much time for Project HOPE at the expense of your job and family," Mendenhall explained.

"I assume you have a plan to offer?" said Susan Standing Bear.

"I do. Starting in 2023, I suggest Project HOPE directors be elected by the international assembly for a term of two years. Ten directors would be selected. The six of you would serve until 2025, then be replaced by new directors from countries around the world. You could run for reelection, for one more term, if you so desired. Each director would be allowed a maximum of two terms," said Mendenhall.

"If we only have a few more years as Project HOPE directors, why spend so much money for a new building?" asked Jim Wildhorse.

"It will be a multipurpose building. It can easily be converted to offices, school rooms, or even new rooms for Great Spirit Bear Lodge. Premier Guyaen has approved the plan, subject to your approval," said DeFord.

Mary Raven said, "I agree with the need to widen the scope of leadership to help provide new ideas. As we graduate from college, start families, and begin our careers, it will be harder for some of us to devote as much time to Project HOPE as we do now. I move we accept the plan offered by Commander Mendenhall and Captain DeFord."

After more discussion and many questions, the motion was seconded and approved. A plan was now in place for a new organizational structure for Project HOPE. Construction and design ideas for the new Project HOPE home were sent to four major architectural firms. The new structure would serve as headquarters until a new board was elected in 2025.

The six initial directors of Project HOPE felt mixed emotions. They were unpaid volunteers.

HOPE had been their consuming passion for three years. However, they needed to start thinking about life after graduating from college. The work of HOPE was of utmost importance. Project HOPE was founded by the six Kitasoo, but the future needed to be directed by the next generation of dedicated leaders.

A TAIL OF THINGS TO COME

Early one morning in late May, Argonaut and his human friend Jason Belliveau were swimming side-by-side in the clear cold water near Orca Lab. Jason was photographing fish and underwater scenes for an article he was writing for Nature Life magazine. Since Argonaut had made peace with all orca in the strait, Jason had no fear of being attacked by the large black dolphins.

The two friends, though very different from one another, both had a love of the ocean waters. They were quiet for long periods as they enjoyed the sights and sounds of Vancouver's Johnstone Strait. Argonaut asked Jason if he could interrupt his photography.

"Of course, old friend," said Jason.

"Do you remember the tail you made for me to hide my identity? It keeps the A on my tail from being visible," Argonaut said.

"I do remember. There was a scientist and a reporter both seeking the identity of the magical whale. We also changed your official name to

Michael in all official records to provide protection for you and your pod," Jason said.

"I need another tail cover made. I need one with the A in the same spot as mine. It will make the whale who wears it look exactly like I did, before I put on my tail cover," Argonaut said.

Jason stopped and stared at Argonaut. He could not believe what Argonaut had just said, using his telepathy.

"You want me to make a tail that looks exactly like your real tail? Why not take off the cover you are wearing now and just be yourself?" Jason asked.

"The new cover is not for me but for another whale. I know it seems confusing. Let me explain. It is important that we are able to cover another whale's tail with a cover that looks like my real tail, including the A. I see a future where two whales are badly hurt. One will almost certainly die. The second whale may also die. I am one of the whales who will be badly hurt. I may be the whale who dies. If the other whale is the one to die, we will put the cover with the A on that whale. People will think Argonaut was killed. That will stop the world from asking about the Inua humpback. My secret will remain safe for now. If I die then there is no secret to keep," said the Inua.

Jason asked Argonaut to explain what he saw of the future.

"It is not perfectly clear. I will tell you what I can see. One humpback will be struck by a boat. He will be severely injured. About the same time another whale will be hurt in a different accident. The second whale will be mortally crippled. I cannot see which one lives or which one dies. I don't know if I am the one who lives or the one who dies or if both whales die," Argonaut said.

"Do you know what causes the accident injuring the whale not struck by the boat," Jason asked.

"No. I know both whales are hurt at almost the same time. I can see humans involved in attempts to save both whales," said Argonaut.

Jason thought about Argonaut's prediction.

"What if you left the sanctuary. Swim away from our home. Would you be safe if you were not here?" Jason asked.

Argonaut swam next to Jason. The humpback carefully extended his pectoral fin so he could touch his closest friend. He had to be careful not to crush Jason with his fin.

"I have a destiny to fulfill. I cannot run and hide every time there is danger. I faced the orca. I faced the great whites. I helped save you, Matt, and many other creatures during the time we have known each other. I feel as if I and the other humpbacks are part of each other's lives. I will not flee our home. Will you help me and have a new tail cover made?" the Inua asked.

"Of course, I will help. I will have another tail cover made. It may not be a perfect fit for a different whale's fluke. Have you thought of that?" Jason said.

"In my vision, the other whale and I are about the same size. If I am the one to die then we do not need the new tail cover. If the other whale dies then the cover will only be needed for a short time," said Argonaut.

"What else can you see of this danger?" asked Jason.

"I see many people, multiple ships, other animals of the land, air, and sea all involved. It will take many days for the final outcome to be known. I think it will be a historic event. You will be there along with Matt, Commander Mendenhall, and Captain DeFord," the Inua explained.

Jason asked, "How much time do we have before these accidents occur?"

Argonaut said, "Within one full cycle of the moon one whale will likely die. It is possible the other whale may not survive."

The two friends continued to swim side-by-side. The sixty-thousand-pound humpback and his human friend were an incredible sight. No two such different creatures had ever communicated like this before, anywhere, ever in the history of the world. What seemed impossible a few years ago now seemed ordinary to them and to those who knew the secret of the Inua.

"Don't worry, Jason. I will do everything in my power to survive. If it is my time to join the whales who are no longer with us, like the Inua Raven Hrafn, my spirit will become a new star. My star, like Hrafn's, would shine on our world forever," Argonaut said to Jason.

Jason had trouble catching his breath. The thought of losing Argonaut was impossible to ponder. The Inua and Jason had become inseparable. These two had shared many adventures, dangers, and excitement. It was as if they were brothers.

Argonaut read Jason's thoughts. The Inua felt the same way. People often dismiss the ability of animals to feel emotions. Argonaut was afraid of losing Jason, Angel, his sons Raven and Jason, and the other members of his pod.

If there was a way to survive, Argonaut would find it.

ARGONAUT AND JASON DISCUSS THE NEW TAIL

TIGERS ARE LURKING NEAR VANCOUVER ISLAND

Raven approached Sitka and asked if he, his younger brother Jason, T-Rex, and T-Rex's son, Little Rex, could begin the ancient ritual of the humpback quest. The quest is a vital part of the maturation process for all young humpback whales.

Sitka agreed to the request. Raven asked his father and mother if the group could start on the quest the following morning.

"Father, I would like to take Jason on this quest. I know it is your right to take your son, but you are always so busy. I would like to help by doing this. Is that OK with you?" Raven asked.

Argonaut remembered just a few years ago that he and Raven had completed the same quest. Knolhval had taken Argonaut on the ancient whale quest many years earlier.

Argonaut looked at Raven and said, "It will be a good thing for you and your brother to share the quest experience. You have our blessing to go on the journey."

The quest is an important part of a young whale's becoming a full member of the pod. Both males and females make the journey at some point in their lives.

As the four whales left the pod, Argonaut had a bad feeling about the trip. He knew Raven and T-Rex were capable of handling difficulties, as they had proven in the past. The anxiety Argonaut felt for his sons and his friends was very troublesome.

The four whales swam north towards Klemtu. Raven explained to the two younger whales they needed to find a raven, a Spirit Bear, an orca, and a salmon.

Raven explained the significance of the many different totems they saw on different First Nation lands.

Once all these creatures were seen, the group could travel west into the ocean depths to visit the site of the sacred ancient humpback whale burial grounds.

"Were you scared when you did the quest with our father?" Jason asked.

"I was excited, nervous, anxious, and a little afraid. I had never left the pod. I had never been away from our mother. It was a very important journey for me. I became much closer to our father.

To experience a quest together bonded us in a way that will forever be in my thoughts. I hope you and I will be even more connected after the quest," Raven said to his brother.

"Our father is the most famous whale any of us have ever known. Even before we knew of his Inua powers, he made me feel safe from danger. I trusted him. I knew he would always protect me," Raven explained.

"I remember my quest. Our kind has made this journey for as long as memory keepers have been telling stories. It is part of what makes us a humpback in these waters. We share this trip with each other as family. We feel more a part of each other than we did before the adventure," T-Rex said to Jason and Little Rex.

They swam in a tight group. They stopped to eat and rest when the young whales were hungry or tired. It took two days to reach Klemtu. The four whales spyhopped and looked at the totem by the Big House. It was the same place Raven had visited with his father a few years earlier.

As the whales swam away from Klemtu both Jason and Little Rex saw a pod of orca. The orca pod was a family of residents. They were feeding on salmon that returned to spawn in the same streams where they were born a few years earlier.

Eagles would swoop down to grab salmon and other fish in their talons.

"This quest seems pretty easy. We have already seen three of the four creatures we must find," said Little Rex.

Raven and T-Rex both smiled and thought to themselves how hard it might be to find the mysterious and elusive Spirit Bear.

For the next three days, the four humpbacks searched day and night in bays and along shores. They could not find a Spirit Bear.

"I am getting tired. Can't we just skip finding the Spirit Bear?" asked Jason.

"Maybe all the Spirt Bears have left and we will never find one," said Little Rex.

"If you want to become a full-grown humpback, we must continue our search until we find the Spirit Bear. The rules of the quest are strict. We will take turns spyhopping. We will swim to Haida Gwaii and then back to Klemtu, if necessary.

We are a team. We will stay the course until we find all the creatures of the totem," T-Rex said.

Finally, after two more days, Jason and Little Rex both spotted a young Spirit Bear standing in a stream trying to catch migrating salmon.

"There is one," they both exclaimed.

"Well done youngsters. Now it is time to start

the long swim to the ancient burial grounds of the humpbacks. You may never show other creatures this site, unless they are on a quest like us. It is where all humpbacks want to come when they die," Raven explained to the two young whales.

The group headed due west into the Pacific Ocean. The sun was rising behind them over the coast of Canada. The whales fed often. They swam at a steady pace. They had many miles to go before they reached the burial cave of the ancients.

Argonaut was following the quest journey of his sons and friends using his Inua powers. He felt a serious threat in the ocean to his family and friends. The sense of danger had been growing with the passing of each day. Both of his sons, T-Rex, and Little Rex were in extreme peril. He did not want to interfere with the quest but, like any father, he was frightened for his sons and his friends.

Argonaut reached out to his friends the great white sharks. He asked if there were any dangers near the west coast of Vancouver.

"We have heard the sound of boats, but they seem far away. We also sense the presence of other large and aggressive sharks, not of our kind, near here," said the elder great white to Argonaut.

"Will you let me know if you sense any danger

to the whales traveling to the humpback burial ground?" Argonaut asked the great whites.

"We are moving further north towards cooler water, but if we sense any danger to your family and friends, we will use our thoughts to reach out," said the great white.

As the whales on the quest were nearing the burial site a large school of frightened bait fish swam in front of them. The bait fish were scared of something. Raven and T-Rex spyhopped to see what was frightening the fish.

Raven said, "Look, there are large shark fins swimming towards us. They cannot be great whites because we have made peace with the great whites."

T-Rex and Raven told the two young sharks to get behind them. There were six large tiger sharks swimming slowly towards the whales.

T-Rex and Raven turned to face the sharks. Tiger sharks are fast, aggressive, and will hunt in a pack to attack larger prey.

Raven told each whale to face in a different direction. The four whales had their tails towards each other. Each whale would be able to see if the sharks were about to attack from the direction they were facing. The four humpbacks agreed to fight to save themselves and each other. T-Rex told the other three to show no fear. He told them to be brave and stay as close together as possible. The giant T-Rex knew the group was safer facing danger as a united fighting force, than if they separated.

The tiger sharks started circling the whales. The circle got smaller and smaller as the sharks studied their prey. The tiger sharks looked for signs of weakness.

Just as the first shark started to make his attack, it was struck by a harpoon. The tiger shark died instantly as it was shot through its heart. Two more sharks were quickly killed by long spears. As the shark carcasses started to sink, they were grabbed by robotic arms attached to two remote-controlled electric submarines. The submarines used a separate arm to cut the fins off the dead sharks. The carcasses of the dead sharks were released and fell to the ocean floor. The fins cut from the sharks were placed in a container attached to the hulls of the small electric shark-killing submarines.

Shark hunters were back in Canadian waters. The ships were being controlled by a satellite flying high overhead. A large container ship nearly fifteen miles away was the base for the unmanned submarines. The large ship was outside Canadian territorial waters.

Raven reached out to his father.

"Have you been tracking what is happening on our quest?" Raven asked Argonaut.

"Of course, I have been tracking your progress. You are my sons and my friends are with you also. Even though you are brave, strong, and intelligent you are always my sons and friends. I worry about both of you, T-Rex, and Little Rex as well," the Inua replied.

"Talk to the tiger sharks. You must tell them to swim deep and fast away from the boats," Raven said.

Argonaut reached out to the tiger sharks who listened to the Inua's voice in their minds. The sleek sharks swam to the south as quickly as they could.

"We are going to destroy these boats before they hurt any more sharks" said the angry Raven.

Raven and Jason swam up to the first submarine on each side. The two whales used all their weight to destroy the fragile electric craft. The light-weight submarine was no match for the two angry humpbacks. The ship was crushed as easily as an empty aluminum can. The wrecked submarine sank in over one-thousand feet of water.

T-Rex and his son approached the second

submarine from the top and the bottom. Their combined weight of over one-hundred-thousand pounds crumpled the sub las easily as a human would destroy a paper bag.

"The sharks are safe. The boats are at the bottom of the ocean. We cannot speak to the sharks. Will you tell them what we have done? Tell them they are welcome here, if they do not enter our sanctuary," Raven thought to his father.

Argonaut did as he was asked. The tiger sharks thanked the whales but they had decided to swim further south. The tigers had a new respect for humpbacks.

The Inua was very angry at the shark hunters. Shark hunters had promised not to return to waters near Vancouver. Argonaut was tempted to reach out and stop the hearts of all the hunters. It would be easy to end the lives of the shark-killers. Argonaut paused before he acted in haste. He would not use his Inua power to kill or injure other creatures, unless it was to save a life.

The Inua spoke with his mind to the crew on the ship. "I am Inua. Again, you have come to my home. You have used your boats and weapons to kill more sharks. You are evil. You have threatened my family. I will not allow you to hunt here. We and the sharks hunt for food to survive. You hunt, not for food, but for profit. I am going to stop each of you from returning here. From this day forward, you will have no memory of being in these waters. You will never return. If you do, your minds will grip your bodies in horrible pain. I, the powerful Inua, will know if you return. Your punishment for breaking my rules will be severe. Leave now or face the wrath of the Inua," Argonaut said.

The ship immediately turned west, away from Vancouver Island. The hunters had heard of the Inua but did not believe the tales. They now knew the truth about the Inua.

The four humpbacks continued to the ancient burial grounds. Raven and T-Rex explained to the two young whales about the long and scary dive to the opening of the cave.

"Trust us young whales. You will be frightened because you have never dived so deeply before. Remember, Raven and I have both already completed this dive. You will be fine. Stay by our side. Are you ready?" T-Rex asked.

The four whales started the long deep dive to the entrance of the ancient burial grounds. When Jason and Little Rex saw the millions of bones in the huge cavern they were in awe. They marveled at the light and fresh air in the vast underwater graveyard.

"I feel the power of our ancestors here. I understand why whales want to lay here for all time once they die," said Little Rex.

Jason nodded his understanding. After a short while all four whales returned to the surface. They began the long journey back to the Johnstone Strait.

The two young whales were brave. They stood alongside their elders in the conflict with the tiger sharks. They did not run when the tiger sharks attacked. They finished their quest. They knew their lives had changed. They were now mature whales ready to take their place among the adults of the pod.

TIGER SHARKS NEAR VANCOUVER ISLAND

MERS EARNS PRAISE

For five years, Jason had been trying to win one of the annual grants offered by the National Geographic Foundation to benefit MERS. Jason hoped a grant would be awarded to the Marine Education Research Society (MERS) to help fund much needed capital equipment acquisitions and to help pay for general operating costs.

Jason completed and submitted a grant application each of the prior five years. He provided photographic evidence of the work done by MERS. He documented MERS efforts that included posting speed warning signs, helping to save injured and trapped marine life, providing educational seminars, teach courses on boater safety, and offering free week-long discovery cruises to first nation students.

If MERS was awarded the grant, they would receive a check for one-hundred-fifty thousand dollars from the National Geographic Foundation.

MERS needed two new boats for volunteers to use while patrolling the straits. New computers, more warning signs to post, and newer dive gear to use on animal rescues were also needed. Rent, utilities, boat fuel, and other costs were increasing each year.

MERS relied on donations and whale sponsorship programs to keep the small non-profit fiscally sound. No government funds were provided to MERS.

In 2022, MERS was notified they were in the top three finalists for the grant.

National Geographic required at least five letters of recommendation from different individuals or groups, not affiliated with MERS. The letters should emphasize the qualities that made MERS deserving of the grant.

The first letter sent was written by former Coast Guard Commander Wild Bill Mendenhall. He spoke of the many marine wildlife rescues MERS had undertaken. He commended MERS for their dedication to the wildlife of the Vancouver Island area.

The next letter was from Matt Hawk. He described the many tireless hours volunteers spent patrolling the waters from Vancouver to Port Hardy helping enforce speed limit zones. He also wrote of the numerous education courses offered to boaters about marine life safety.

Captain Jim Hawk told the foundation he had been working with MERS for over twenty-five years in identifying orca and humpbacks for classification purposes. Photographs of the mammals were necessary to help trace migration patterns. MERS volunteers were spending thousands of hours each year identifying, tracking, and cataloging wildlife of the area.

The most powerful recommendation letters were the six written by the Kitasoo directors of Project HOPE. Each Kitasoo told of their adventure aboard the Orcella 2. It was during this trip they first became interested in saving the world from destruction due to pollution and climate change. From the MERS sponsored trip, the group was inspired to start what is now the world's largest organization fighting to save the planet. Without MERS there would be no Project HOPE.

Based on the letters of recommendation to the National Geographic Foundation Board, MERS was awarded the 2022 grant. The funds could be used for any of the goals of MERS.

Jason and the other MERS volunteers and staff were ecstatic. More volunteers could be recruited since there were more boats for patrol duty. Additional courses, both live and online, could be offered for volunteers to learn about saving the local marine life. The operating budget could provide for long delayed purchases of boats, new computers, desks, signs, and general supplies.

A ceremony was held at the Big House on Klemtu. The National Geographic Foundation director presented the check to Jason, as the MERS representative. The story of the grant was carried throughout Canada and around the world as part of Project HOPE communiques to all the group chapters.

It seems like a small step, but MERS, like so many other groups, is waging the good fight to save our planet. The Kitasoo all surrounded Jason, who was an adopted Kitasoo tribe member. They sang native songs and danced long into the evening. It seemed fitting that the Kitasoo had helped MERS since it was MERS volunteers who had planted the seed for the growth of Project HOPE in the hearts and minds of the young directors.

WHALE GAMES

Every generation of humpback whales has to learn certain skills. Hunting for food, practicing echo location, listening for and avoiding boats, tracking objects exact location by spyhopping, looking for star formations, migration routes, and much more.

Humpies are born with certain abilities. Like humans, they need to practice to perfect their natural talents.

One of the most important parts of a humpback whale's life is singing. The songs of humpbacks have been recorded and played for many years throughout the world. There are many reasons whales sing. Whales can help find other whales by singing out and listening for a response. Songs can attract mates. Sometimes, like humans, whales sing to express emotions.

Argonaut is considered one of the best singer other whales have ever heard. He asked all the younger whales of the Sitka pod to join him in a quiet bay away from the main channel of the

Johnstone Strait.

"Today, we will learn songs and practice our singing. We will have fun. When we are done each of you will sing for the group," Argonaut said to the young whales gathered by his side.

"First, you must surface and fill your lungs through your blowholes. When you are ready, dive down to where I will be swimming. We will each take turns making sounds. The idea is to move air in the area behind your tongue. You do not need to open your mouth. It is more of a deep vibration. You can change the sound by moving more or less air behind your tongue. Have fun. Just practice making any sounds you want. Ready?" Argonaut asked his young class.

Each of the youngsters rose to the surface and took in air. As they swam to Argonaut, they all began making different sounds. Some were higher, some were lower, some were shorter, and some were longer.

When the students finished their first lesson, Argonaut smiled and said, "Well done young whales."

They practiced singing again and again. With each session, the songs became longer, louder, and more beautiful. After three hours of practice, they were ready for their solo performances.

All the young whales, both male and female, sang in turn. Argonaut praised each calf as they finished.

After the last whale sang, Argonaut said, "Now we will play a game. We will all go the surface, take a deep breath, then swim back to me. When we are together you must each close your eyes. I will reach out using my mind and ask each of you, one at a time, to sing your best song. The others will guess who is singing. It is important to know, when we are away from each other, whose song we hear. This will be fun but it is also important. Someday your songs may save your life or the life of another one of our pod," said Argonaut.

The group rose to the surface, filled their lungs, and swam to Argonaut. He took turns, asking each whale to sing. After each song, the others had to guess the singer. With a little practice all the whales were able to correctly guess which whale was singing.

"You all did wonderfully. I may no longer be the most famous singer in our pod. I think you are the best young whale song makers I have ever heard. Practice every day. Did you notice anything special about the songs we sang?" Argonaut asked.

A young female named Patty said, "We all sound a little bit like each other. Not exactly the same, but close. I think I could tell a song from our pod from other whale pods."

"You are exactly right. One way we know our family is by the songs we sing. If we go to a new place and we sing, we should then listen. We may hear others of our family who sound like us," said Argonaut.

The next day, Argonaut gathered his young class together and said, "Today we will play a new game. I want each of you to turn your tails towards me. I will swim away and hide from you. Use your echo locating senses to find me. Do not swim too far apart from each other. It is important to be able to locate any object by echo sounds, when it is too dark to see. When I am ready, I will send a signal to your thoughts. We will play the game several times. Each time I will hide in an area that is harder to locate. First, use your echo skill to sense what size and shape I am. When I am hiding, look for the same size and shape."

Once the youngsters had a good sense of Argonaut's shape and size, they turned away from him. He swam about one-half mile away and hid around the corner of a bay. When he was ready, he sent a signal for the class to find him. Some whales went south, others went north. Soon they were spread out too far. Argonaut gave them hints of his location. Eventually, all of the young calves found him.

"We will try again. This time I will be farther away, but I will make a soft sound to help you get the general direction of my location," Argonaut told his students.

On the next attempt, the Inua swam about one-mile due east towards mainland Canada. He hid behind a small island. Once he was ready, he told the calves to hunt for him. He made low sounds of a song. Between his song and their echo locations they found him easily.

"Remember, if you are ever lost, sing and others of your family will be able to find you more quickly," said Argonaut.

On the third day of class, Argonaut gathered the group and said, "It is important to understand about the dangers in our sanctuary. Boats can kill us. If you hear a boat you should swim away and dive deep. You must be very careful not to surface near a boat."

They swam near the shore of orca rubbing beach and listened for boats. When a British Columbia Ferry was approaching, Argonaut told the class to listen carefully.

"Do you hear that sound? That is danger. Never, ever get close to a boat. You can be crushed or cut. Close your eyes. Feel the wave on your skin as the boat moves. When you think you know which direction the boat is coming from, use one of your pectoral fins to point where the boat is," Argonaut told the youngsters.

They listened carefully. Each young humpback pointed due south. It was the direction of the approaching ferry.

"Well done. Now that we know where the boat is, let's swim closer to shore and stay away from the channel. If we were not close to shore and it was deep enough, we might be able to dive and escape. It is important to never surface or breach unless you are sure there are no boats nearby. You must always pay attention and always be alert. When you eat or play do not get distracted from listening for boats. Boats cannot hear or see us underwater. Even though humans on boats mean us no harm, these boats can easily kill any of us," Argonaut told his students.

Argonaut sensed a large bait ball close by and told the calves to go and have fun feeding. He was very proud of them.

Although these were games, they were also important life lessons to these young whales. Being taught by the famous Inua Argonaut made a great impression on the calves. For the rest of their lives, they would often speak of how they had learned from the Inua Argonaut to sing, echo locate, and be safe from boats.

THE INUA SPEAKS

As the Project HOPE directors were flying to Ottawa, for their presentations to the combined bodies of the bicameral Canadian Legislature, Jill thought how much progress they had made in the last few years. From being high school students on the remote island of Klemtu they had matured to being speakers before their country's legislature. Project HOPE just surpassed thirty-two million members and was steadily growing. A new office building was under construction on Klemtu. Commander Mendenhall and Captain DeFord had organized the finances, operating structure, advertising, and all other administrative aspects of the group. The directors could entirely focus on dealing with regional and national issues critical to saving the planet.

Premier Guyaen met the Project HOPE group at the Ottawa airport. He escorted them to his official residence. A donor meet and greet event was planned for that evening to help raise money for Project HOPE. Donors from across Canada and several other countries attended the event.

The Premier rose and addressed the group.

"We are honored to have with us this evening the six original members of Project HOPE. What started in a quiet village on an island in western Canada is now a major international force for change. The six young Kitasoo you see here tonight may be our best chance for implementing changes needed to save earth. It is an honor to know these young adults who have dedicated their lives to Project HOPE. I encourage each of you to contribute generously to the cause. Thank you," said the Premier.

Charles Windsong was selected to speak to the donor group. Before helping start Project HOPE he had been a quiet and shy person. Being a leader of a huge international organization helped him become more outgoing. He was now accustomed to public speaking.

"Premier Guyaen, honored guests, and friends. Thank you for the opportunity to be here tonight. We are waging a battle for the very life of our planet. We face great obstacles, such as corporate polluters, people who deny science, inertia, fear of change, and many other problems. We have seen the results of humanity's inaction. Global ice sheets are melting. Ocean temperatures are rising. Water levels are increasing with alarming speed.

Wildfires in the western United States and Australia, and increased hurricane and typhoon activity are all results of global warming. Huge numbers of bird deaths are being recorded. Whales and other wildlife are acting in strange ways. The quality of our air is getting worse. Our reliance of fossil fuels is not abating quickly enough. More than eight-billion people on earth are using up scare resources like clean air and water at an accelerating rate. Species extinction is forever and this process is accelerating. Massive economic crises are certain to occur. We need to fight influence with power. We need to combat these problems with more voices calling for change. We need you to act, vote, and encourage others to join us in meeting the goals of Project HOPE. Thank you," said Charles.

A long round of applause followed the speech. Large donation checks to Project HOPE were written. After a long day, the group was finally able to get some rest. Tomorrow they would address the Canadian governmental officials.

The next morning the six Kitasoo left for the legislative offices accompanied by Premier Guyaen. They were ushered to a dais in front of the assembled body.

Jill rose to speak. "Good morning. Many of you

know of Project HOPE. Some of you have voted to support legislation aimed at fighting pollution and controlling global warming. We six are just the spokespersons for a much larger group. Hundreds of millions of people around the world are listening. They are waiting for you, and others like you, to act in a clear and decisive manner. We are losing the battle against pollution and climate change. If we lose the war then your children and grandchildren may not have a planet that supports life. There is no work more important than saving earth. You must not fail, because if you do fail then we all die. We each prepared remarks for you today but decided there is one important voice that may have more impact than our words. If you will quiet your minds, a friend of ours wants to speak with you. Please listen."

"I am one of the ancient Inua. My name is not important. I know each of you can hear me. I am one of the many creatures who will become extinct if you fail to act to save earth. The young people standing before you are brave and smart. These brave and fearless warriors are fighting for all of us. Listen to these young humans. Listen to the scientists who speak the truth. There is much you do not know about the damage being done to the world we share. Know this, time is running out. I have a family that will die if you do not hurry. Inua cannot lie. I need the same air to breathe that you require. I am but one, you influence many. Only you can save us. What are you waiting for? Have you not seen the smoke, the melting ice, the warming waters, and all other changes the Kitasoo speak of? Please, before it is too late, work hard to save earth for your kind and mine," Argonaut said.

The legislature erupted. Everyone was on their feet. All the legislators were speaking at once. The speaker of the House of Lords gaveled for quiet. Finally, order was restored. The speaker turned to the Kitasoo.

"Do you know this Inua who has just spoken to us?" the speaker asked.

"We do," all six Project HOPE directors replied.

"Can or will you tell us about this being?" the speaker asked.

Susan Standing Bear said, "We have sworn to keep the Inua's identity secret. To protect the Inua's safety is very important to us. You all heard the voice of the Inua. There are many things in the world we don't yet understand. We do understand and believe the words of our friend the Inua. We beg you to heed his warning and our pleas before time runs out."

Slowly, applause started with a few members

of the legislature. Soon every member was applauding with great enthusiasm. The Inua had made an impact. The Kitasoo now had a model to reach other government officials and major corporations.

Premier Guyaen escorted the Project HOPE directors back to the Ottawa airport.

"You did more today, with the help of your Inua friend, than all the people, groups, and initiatives that have gone before you. Maybe someday, I will have a chance to meet the Inua," the Premier said.

"Thank you, sir. I think the Inua would like to meet you as well. For now, the Inua desires to stay safe by remaining anonymous. More work needs to be done by all governments. Canada can set the example," Joan Redclaw responded to the Premier.

As the jet carrying the six directors left Ottawa for Vancouver, the group high-fived each other.

"Argonaut did a great job. He made a difference. If we can repeat this effort in other countries, we may be able to finally have a real impact," Mary Raven said.

It had been a long and challenging trip. The young Project HOPE directors were soon fast asleep as the Air Canada jet flew towards western Canada.

Argonaut explained to Sitka and the entire pod

what happened in Ottawa.

"Is it safe for you to be more exposed to the world?" asked Knolhval.

"If the humans do not act to save our home, we may all perish. It's worth the risk, if we succeed. We all want the young Kitasoo to change the world before it is too late," said Argonaut.

The Canadian legislature was true to its word. New laws were enacted within days of Argonaut's communication.

Air quality regulations were strengthened. New recycling requirements were enacted. More stringent miles-per-gallon (kilometers-per-gallon in Canada) were legislated starting with the next vehicle production year. Geothermal, wind, and solar power generating companies would receive new tax credits. Fossil fuel companies would be charged heavy surtaxes. Funds for additional research inti new production methods were allocated. Much more work needed to be done. Canada was now the world's leader in efforts to save earth from climatic and pollution catastrophes. It was fitting that the home country of the Kitasoo was now the most prominent force for change of any government in the world.

In recognition of their efforts, the six Kitasoo Project HOPE directors were awarded Canada's highest civilian honor. They were each to be honored with the Meritorious Service Cross. They were the youngest individuals to ever receive the award in Canada's history.

The world was taking notice of what Project HOPE was accomplishing. Perhaps, just perhaps, there was time left to save earth.

Word of the Inua's telepathic communication spread throughout the entire world.

Brigitte Fisher smiled at what her friend Argonaut and the Kitasoo were doing. She knew the Inua's secret, but it was safe with her. Soon, she and the Inua's paths would cross again.

ARGONAUT AND JASON ANSWER A DISTRESS CALL

June is a beautiful time of the year in the straits of Vancouver. The air is clean, bait fish are plentiful, the salmon are swimming upstream to spawn, and the bears are eating their fill. Sedge grass, berries, and salmon are all critical parts of a bear's diet. A balanced diet is essential for bears to produce offspring.

Eagles catch fish with ease. The sea lions, always on the lookout for the transient orca, are constantly feeding. The sea lions are storing food they eat as fat for the cold winter months ahead.

Matt was busy leading tours aboard the Orcella 2. Jason was photographing the many underwater wonders of the straits. Both of the friends were volunteering for MERS, as much as possible.

Argonaut and his pod were feeding heavily in preparation for their annual winter migration to Hawaii.

The new Project HOPE building was taking shape on Klemtu. The waiting list was long for visitors hoping to get a chance to stay at Spirit Bear Lodge. Spotting a Spirit Bear was becoming more common on many people's bucket list.

The whale watching ship, Leviathan, was filled with visitors on both the morning and afternoon trips from Telegraph Cove. Ninety people on each trip lined the decks looking for whales, orca, sea lions, eagles, black bears and dolphins.

Commander Pierstorff had recently retired from the Canadian Coast Guard. She volunteered her services to MERS and Orca Lab. Both organizations welcomed her with great anticipation. The Canadian Coast Guard Commander was a lifelong wildlife preservationist. Her vast knowledge of the waters around Vancouver was legendary. Her advanced technology skills were a much-needed addition to the capabilities of both MERS and Orca Lab.

Captain Bruce Brient was promoted to Commander of the western Canadian Coast Guard fleet. Four new ships and two new helicopters had recently been added to the fleet's equipment. Every year more tourists, cruise ships, and fishermen were using the straits near Vancouver. Illegal drug smuggling continued to be a problem that kept the Coast Guard busy.

As Argonaut and the pod were feeding near the

southern end of the Johnstone Strait, Argonaut heard a call for help from animals he had never heard before.

Based on his echo location skills, Argonaut knew the distressed animals were located about twenty miles south of the pod's current location and heading north. Argonaut asked Sitka if he, Knolhval, and T-Rex could respond to the distress calls. Maybe there was something they could do to help. Sitka approved their search for the troubled creatures.

As the three whales swam south, Argonaut reached out to Jason. The Sadie Princess had been to Vancouver for repairs. Jason was on his way back to Port Hardy aboard his boat.

"Jason, I have felt the cries for help from a group of animals that I think are located between you and where we are. Do you see any animals in trouble?" said the Inua to his friend.

"I am about ten miles south of Nanaimo and heading north. I have not seen anything unusual. Are you sure the calls for help are coming from the straits?" Jason asked.

"I am certain of the location. It sounds as if there are many voices crying out in fear. Keep going north in your boat as we swim towards you. We should meet soon and hopefully find the frightened animals. I have never heard voices like these. I think they are some kind of whale. The voices are not orca, not dolphin, and certainly not humpbacks. What other kind of whale could it be?" asked the Inua.

"There are other types of whales that migrate from the Artic towards the far south and then return. They never come into the straits near us. Pods of gray whales stay far out to sea. The grays, under normal conditions, never even approach the coast. If the voices you hear are, in fact, gray whales something must be terribly wrong. More and more of these whales are beaching themselves along the coast of the United States. I am not sure if we can help these animals. I agree, we must do our best to save them from danger. Fewer and fewer of these whales are being spotted. There is a decline in new offspring. The grays that I have seen in recent years appear thin, malnourished, and sick. I will let you know if I spot them," Jason said.

Argonaut, T-Rex, and Knolhval swam south as fast as they could. Argonaut was probing the minds of the frightened animals. He told them help was on the way. Argonaut heard the plaintive cries for help. Even his Inua powers were not able to calm the frightened animals.

Just as the humpies saw the gray whales, they

also saw Jason arriving on the Sadie Princess. The boat and humpbacks approached the floundering gray whales cautiously.

Argonaut reached out to all the grays and said, "Friends, I am Argonaut the Inua. I, my two whale friends, and my human friend have come to help you. Can you tell me what is wrong?"

All the whales started thinking their responses at once. Argonaut asked the oldest whale to speak first. He wanted to understand the situation clearly.

"Inua, we have been traveling for a long, long time. We are trying to make our way back to our home in the north. The area we seek has cooler and cleaner water and more food. Each year more of us die. We are having fewer calves. The journey to our colder home takes longer. We do not have the strength to swim and feed as quickly as we did in my youth. We have been swimming in circles. Some of us cannot dive or swim in a straight line. We easily become confused. It took all our strength to enter these waters. We do not come as enemies. I am afraid if we do not get help, we may all die," said the eldest gray whale.

Argonaut explained to Jason, T-Rex, and Knolhval what the gray whale had said. He asked Jason if he knew what was causing the grays to be in such distress.

"More and more gray whales are beaching themselves. We are not sure why. They are dying of malnutrition and not producing many calves. There are many theories. Some say, it is pollution in the water. People claim that plastic left in the water is entering the internal systems of these whales and it affects their brains and other organs. Other scientists claim the bait fish have become harder for the grays to find and eat because of over fishing by humans. Like you, the grays have echolocation. It is thought by some scientists that due to the number of boats in the water using sonar the grays are becoming confused, lost, and disoriented. It may also be true that huge solar flare activity could be disrupting the magnetic field of the earth causing the whales to beach. Solar flare cycles appear in eleven-year episodes and this is a peak season," Jason said.

Jason called Professor John Leibach to ask if he had any ideas how to help a floundering pod of gray whales that had strayed into the Johnstone Strait.

Leibach responded, "It is hard to tell exactly what is wrong with these particular whales. The species is in grave danger. If they swam through polluted waters or ate polluted fish they may survive living in clean water and eating clean food.

The grays need to stay calm, eat healthy food, and live in cleaner water, at least until they regain their health. The trick is to keep them safe until they can improve their condition. They will not survive if they beach themselves."

"Thanks, John. I will ask some friends to help. We will do our best to save these grays," Jason said.

Argonaut listened to the conversation between Jason and the professor. He explained the facts to his father and T-Rex.

"What can we do to help, son?" asked Knolhval.

"We need to move the whales out of the main channel and into a shallow bay. If they stay here, they could be hit by boats. We must stop them from beaching. We also must get them some food," Argonaut said to his father, T-Rex, and Jason.

Argonaut reached out with his Inua powers and entered the minds of each of the gray whales. He calmed their thoughts. He used his Inua voice to settle their fears. He told them he and his friends were here to help. The grays had to trust the humpbacks and their human friend, if they wanted to survive.

"Jason, turn your boat around and start slowly towards Isolation Sound. T-Rex, follow Jason's boat. Father, you and I will swim on either side of the pod. I will ask the grays to follow Jason and T-

Rex while you and I keep the pod together. If you see any stragglers let me know and I will bring them back into the group. Is everyone ready?" asked Argonaut.

The Sadie Princess started slowly, followed by T-Rex. The grays were nervous, but the Inua had helped calm them. The grays sensed Argonaut's tremendous power. The grays instinctively trusted the Inua. The group made its way towards Isolation Sound. Like young ducks following their mother, the procession moved slowly north.

Argonaut reached out to Sitka and explained what was happening.

"Is there anything we can do to help?" Sitka asked.

"I would like the pod to drive as much bait fish as possible into the waters near Isolation Sound. We will be there in a short while. These grays need food and safety. They need to rest and regain their energy," said Argonaut.

"We will do as you ask," Sitka replied.

The grays moved slowly. With the sound of the Sadie Princess as a guide, and with the voice of Argonaut in their heads, they swam towards the waiting Sitka pod.

At last the grays made their way into Isolation Sound. Sitka and the other humpies had driven schools of bait fish into the sound for the grays. The starving gray whales ate as much as they could. The krill were plentiful.

The oldest gray spoke to Argonaut, "Inua, we are very thankful for the help of you, your pod, and your human friend. The food provided by your pod has saved us for now. May we stay here for a few days until we regain our strength?"

Argonaut spoke so all of the grays, his pod, and Jason could hear.

"You are safe from danger here. We are at peace with the orca. The dolphins are our friends. Boats will not harm you in the shallow waters of this sound. We will help you feed until your strength returns. The water here is clean. You are welcome to remain with us until you are ready to start your journey back to your home in the north," Argonaut said.

The gray whales stayed in the sound for almost two weeks. Every day, Sitka's pod helped find food for the grays. Argonaut's presence was a calming influence. The grays soon were ready to begin their journey back to the Artic.

Argonaut and the entire pod traveled with the grays to the northern entrance of Johnstone Strait. As the grays slowly swam north, Argonaut knew how important his work as an Inua was to his pod and other creatures. It never ceased to amaze the Inua how busy life was in this small corner of the world.

As the grays swam away, Sitka's pod returned to the waters near Telegraph Cove.

Argonaut told Jason the grays had started their journey home.

"I will ask the Canadian Coast Guard and US Navy to keep a lookout for the grays. Hopefully, they will make the journey home safely. You did a remarkable job," Jason replied.

"I had help from you, T-Rex, Raven, my father, and the entire pod. We make a great team," said the Inua.

Argonaut reached out to the Kitasoo. He explained what had happened to the gray whales. It was another story the Project HOPE directors could spread about damage being done to marine life.

NEW SCHOOL FOR THE KITASOO

Both retired teachers who came to Klemtu three years ago were on vacation in Florida. LeeAnne Gionet and Sarah Clark had been volunteering their time to help the Kitasoo Project HOPE directors stay current with their studies as the project grew from a start-up to a worldwide phenomenon.

The two friends enjoyed living with the Kitasoo. After the Project HOPE founders left for college, the teachers had stayed in Klemtu and tutored other Kitasoo students. The teachers were instrumental in helping the tribe fight COVID-19. As trained first aid responders, the two teachers helped save many lives.

Chief White Feather asked Wild Bill Mendenhall and Captain DeFord to join the tribe elders in the Big House for a meeting. The two former Coast Guard officers entered the Big House. They saw a model of a new building sitting on a table in the middle of the dance area. They both took time to study the architect's rendering and saw the name on the building. They looked at each other and smiled.

They took their seats behind the elders. Chief White Feather rose to speak.

"Two teachers, LeeAnne and Sarah, who came to Klemtu have been helping us for three years. They saved my life when I had the virus. They enabled our young people to prepare for college. They became a part of our family. We have asked the provincial government for funds to build a new school. Klemtu is growing. More tourists are arriving to see the Spirit Bear and stay in our lodge. Project HOPE has brought more people to live and work among us. Our fellow First Nation peoples on Bella Bella, Bella Coola, and Haida Gwaii have asked us to allow our two teachers to work part-time with their students, as well as those on Klemtu.

"If the government approves funding, we propose building a new six-room schoolhouse that will include a computer lab and other advanced equipment. We want to help all our students do better academically. We want to attract more teachers to our island. We need a more modern school.

"The tribal council voted to name the building the Gionet and Clark Education Center in honor of our two friends. We also voted to invite them to become part of our tribe.

"If they are willing, we want them to stay with us, and with our fellow tribes, building a better educational environment for our young people."

Captain DeFord rose to speak, "You and your people are wise. Education is the key to the future. Commander Mendenhall and I will do all we can to help with the school."

"My daughter operated on the provincial governor several years ago when he had a medical emergency in Nanaimo. I will ask her to contact the governor and voice her support for the school," Mendenhall said.

Everyone agreed with the ideas of building a new school and adopting the two teachers into the tribe. The teachers were due back from vacation in three days. There was much to do. A large party was planned. Guests from neighboring islands were invited for the initiation of the teachers into the Kitasoo tribe. Jason and Matt were invited to the celebration. Jason had been adopted by the Kitasoo two years earlier.

Mendenhall texted LeeAnne and told her, upon their arrival, he would pick she and Sarah up at the Vancouver airport. He would fly them in his helicopter back to Klemtu.

When Mendenhall and the teachers arrived at Klemtu a large crowd started cheering. The teachers were taken aback.

"What is going on? Is there a wedding or a birthday we missed?" Sarah asked.

The chief approached the teachers. He instructed them to follow him into the Big House. The space was full of cheering First Nation people from several different island tribes.

There was a stage with two chairs. The chief asked the teachers to sit. He explained the governor had approved the funding for a new school on Klemtu. Chief White Feather had the model for the new school brought on stage. The two teachers saw the building was named for them. They were overcome with emotion.

"We hope to adopt you both into our tribe as members of the Kitasoo Xai'xais. If you accept, we ask you to stay with us and teach our students for as long as you want. You are welcome to spend the rest of your days here among us. Other tribes need teachers like you. We are willing to share your many talents with our brothers and sisters in neighboring tribes. From this day forward, you will always be Kitasoo. We hope you will be the first of many teachers from outside our tribes, to live among us and become part of our family," said the chief.

Through their tears, both teachers accepted

the invitation from Chief White Feather.

The teachers were each given a hand-woven blanket with their new tribal symbols. LeeAnne was the Eagle. Sarah was the Dolphin. There was much dancing and singing. The party lasted long into the night.

The Kitasoo had two new members of their family. The First Nation was excited to have two permanent, full-time teachers to help the students of their tribe be the best they could be. No longer would students have to leave home for a good education.

MORE MEMORY KEEPER STORIES TO LEARN

Sitka asked Argonaut to swim with her. The pod was feeding. There were no dangers nearby. She said, "We have not been working on our memory stories. Being an Inua has kept you busy. While life is calm, let us make time for you to learn a few more lessons from the ancients."

"You are the matriarch. You have my loyalty and my attention. Please begin. I will learn from your wisdom," said the Inua.

Sitka spoke, "Many seasons ago there was a famous city high on a hill. Our kind was treated with respect and dignity by the people of this beautiful city. All creatures of the sea were safe. It is said that the humans who lived in this city were the kindest, bravest, and most wonderful people the world had ever known. In human words, the city was called Atlantis."

"Where is this incredible city?" Argonaut asked.

"Legends say there was a great shaking under the land around Atlantis. Because of the terrible quaking, the ocean swallowed this famous city and all its people. I do not know the location of the lost city of Atlantis. The memory keepers say it was a place of many wonders," Sitka told her young friend.

"Do you think we could find this lost city?" Argonaut asked.

"For more seasons than we can count, humans have been searching for Atlantis. No one has found the city beneath the sea. Perhaps no one ever will. The story is important for us to remember. There was a time when all people of this one city were kind to us. All other creatures of the sea were respected and treated with dignity. Perhaps, one day in the future, we will see more cities like Atlantis," Sitka said to Argonaut.

"There are good people trying to help us. The young Kitasoo, Jason, Matt, Commander Mendenhall, Commander Pierstorff, and Captain DeFord work very hard to save us from the dangers that could harm us," Argonaut told his matriarch.

Sitka sighed and said, "That is true, but it may be too little and too late."

Argonaut asked Sitka to tell him another story from the ancients.

"In a land further away than our winter home, there was a large group of brothers. One of the sons was his father's favorite. The favoritism made another brother mad. The angry brother took the favored son out on a boat and tried to drown him. The good brother prayed to the great spirits of his world. The spirits sent a humpback whale, like us, to save him and take him back to land. This is the story of Paikea as told by our memory keepers," Sitka told Argonaut.

"How do you know so many different stories?" Argonaut asked his matriarch.

"I have been learning my whole life to be a memory keeper, just as you are learning. I have a good memory. I'm not Inua, but I do my best to remember all I have been taught," Sitka said.

Argonaut asked Sitka for one more memory before they rejoined the pod.

"In the long ago past there was a very famous king. He had power, wealth, and a large tribe that worshiped him. The great king was very lucky. His land grew enough food to feed all his people and their many animals. He became arrogant with his success. He decided to grow enough food to feed the entire world. The great spirit became angry at the pride of the king. The spirit sent a giant humpback onto the king's land. The great whale ate all the food the king had grown. The king asked the whale if there were more creatures like him. The whale told the king there were seventy-thousand more whales just as large. The king was humbled. He learned a valuable lesson in humility. No one can feed the entire world," Sitka said.

Argonaut thought of the story of the famous king for a long time.

"Maybe I can learn something from this story. I am but one whale. No matter how hard I try, I cannot save every creature. I cannot possibly help every human or animal. Maybe like the king of the memory story, I should be humbler and not try to do everything," said the Inua.

Sitka smiled and said to Argonaut, "That is a good lesson to learn. Do all you can, be the best Inua you can be, but remember, you are just one whale. There is so much you have already done. I sense you have much good left to do. Be kind to yourself my young friend. Do not take on the burdens of the whole world."

The two whales slowly swam back to the pod. Argonaut was always happy to see Angel, Raven, and the others he cared for so much. He might not be able to save everyone, but he would fight to the death to save these whales.

MATT FINDS A FIRST MATE

Newly promoted one-star General Angela Choate was returning to her station in Seattle aboard a Delta airlines flight from Washington, DC.

General Choate had attended her promotion ceremony at the Pentagon. She was given command of the 62nd Airlift Wing stationed at McChord Field south of Tacoma, Washington. McChord Field is the home of the 62nd Airlift Wing, Air Mobility Command. The field's primary mission being worldwide strategic airlift. With this promotion, the general would be an administrator and no longer flying her beloved jets.

Choate had mixed emotions. She had trained as a combat pilot and served several tours in the middle east. She had been in the United States Air Force for over twenty-five years. Since graduating from the Air Force Academy she had been a fighter pilot during her entire enlistment. The adrenaline rush from flying her jet "Relentless" was like nothing else in the world. Her promotion to a desk job was necessary to advance her career. She was not thrilled with the change.

On the flight back to the northwest coast she read the airline inflight magazine. The general saw an article about whale-watching tours aboard the Orcella 2. The tours were led by Matt Hawk, from his family's home in Telegraph Cove on Vancouver Island in British Columbia. General Choate remembered fondly her flights helping to save the whale that was kidnapped from the straits of Vancouver. She also remembered her part in helping to destroy the attacking unmanned submarine sent by North Korea to kill humpbacks.

The general had two weeks leave before assuming her new command. On a lark, she called the tour operation number listed in the article. She happened to reach Matt Hawk.

"Hello. This is United States Air Force General Angie Choate calling from Seattle. I saw the article about your tour operations. Do you have space available for one more guest on a tour in the next two weeks?" she said.

Matt knew about the general helping save Angel and her efforts that destroyed the attacking submarine. The information was top secret so he could not talk about his knowledge of the events.

"General, I know a friend of yours, Wild Bill Mendenhall. He speaks very highly of you. We have a tour starting the day after tomorrow. Due to a last-minute cancellation, we have room for one more guest aboard ship. It would be an honor to have you join us. Can you be in Telegraph Cove by tomorrow evening?" Matt asked.

"I will catch a flight from SEA-TAC to Vancouver. From Vancouver I will ask your Coast Guard to transport me to Port Hardy. I will rent a car in Port Hardy and drive to Telegraph Cove. I should be there before 7 PM tomorrow night," General Choate said.

"Great. We will hold dinner for you. Your room will be ready. I look forward to meeting you. See you tomorrow night. Have a safe trip," Matt said.

True to her word, General Choate arrived in Telegraph Cove a little before 7 PM on Saturday night. There was a full tour set to leave on the Orcella 2 the following morning. After introductions, the group met for dinner. Matt went over the daily routine, schedules, and safety precautions. He showed a video of what the guests could expect on their excursion. Jason agreed to help Matt with this tour. Jason often volunteered to speak to guests about the marine biology of the sanctuary.

The next morning, after a wonderful breakfast, the group walked to the harbor and boarded the

Orcella 2. As the ship left the harbor, the boat was surrounded by a huge school of pacific white-sided dolphin. Several pods of orca were nearby. The guests watched a single humpback breach thirty times in one hour.

Matt lowered the hydrophones into the water so everyone could listen to the mysterious songs of the humpbacks. Jason spent time explaining to the group what was happening to the environment of the Johnstone Strait due to rising sea temperatures and pollution.

"Each generation of whale is more polluted than the previous. Each spawn of salmon is more polluted than the ones before. Water temperature changes are so dramatic that great white sharks and tiger sharks are right outside the northern harbor of Vancouver Island. Bear hibernation patterns are changing. Bird populations have been seriously affected. We are in a dangerous time," Jason explained.

It is hard to imagine, when you see the pristine beauty of the area around Telegraph Cove, how fragile the environment is and how close to the precipice the world has come.

The general asked Jason if there was anything that could be done to save the animals.

"There is a group called Project HOPE that is

trying desperately to influence governments, corporations, and individuals. In fact, your friend Bill Mendenhall is one of the leading administrators of the group," Jason explained.

"I have read about Project HOPE. They appear to be led by a remarkable group of young First Nation people," Choate replied.

Jason told the group Project HOPE had begun as the result of a cruise on the Orcella 2, much like the one they were on. Matt and Jason were very proud to be associated with the start of Project HOPE.

Each day the group saw many different types of wildlife. Eagles were catching salmon. They went north and were fortunate to see a young Sprit Bear by the shore of Haida Gwaii. Humpbacks surfaced right next to the Orcella 2. It was a wonderful week. The general, for the first time in decades, was relaxed. She was truly living in the moment. She felt a strong attraction to the bays, inlets, islands, and especially the animals of the area. The more she reflected on her life the more she realized how little she had done, other than be in the military. She wondered if it was time to make a change. Perhaps she should try something different.

On the last night of the expedition, at the final dinner, Matt asked the guests if they had any questions.

"How do you manage all the chores necessary to keep these wonderful expeditions running?" Choate asked.

"I have part-time cooks help prepare meals. Jason helps whenever he can. Sometimes I hire temporary crew members to assist with the tours. It is an exhausting schedule, but I love the work. For six months a year this is all I do. I need more crew, but not many people want to live in Telegraph Cove since we are so remote," Matt said.

The next morning, General Choate approached Matt. She handed him her resume. She was an excellent diesel-engine mechanic. She understood navigation. She spent many summers in the waters of New England sailing and working on boats. She was certified in all levels of first-aid. She was a licensed PADI master scuba diver.

"This is very impressive. Why are you showing it to me?" Matt asked.

"I am applying to be your first-mate aboard the Orcella 2. If you hire me, I will retire from the Air Force. I can rent a small condo in Telegraph Cove. I will work with you during your tour season, then travel the world the remainder of the year," she said.

Matt was stunned. She had all the

qualifications he needed to help run his company. "I cannot afford to pay a general. I am paying my parents what I owe for purchasing the Orcella 2. Your pay would be lousy and the work hours long. You would not be in command. You will need to take orders. Even with your remarkable credentials you still have a lot to learn," Matt told Choate.

"I have taken orders all my life and worked hard my entire career. I want to be in the open air, among the wonders of this marine sanctuary. I would also like to help with Project HOPE. Between my military retirement income and earnings from my investments, I am financially secure. I will work for minimum wage, if you are willing to take chance on me," she said.

"When can you start?" Matt asked.

"I will resign my commission and file my retirement papers. I will report for work two weeks from today. Do we have a deal?" she asked.

Matt smiled and shook her hand.

"Welcome to the Orcella 2 Expedition Company. You have a lot to learn but I have a feeling we will work well together," Matt said.

True to her word, two weeks later Angie Choate rented a small condominium near the harbor. She began the hard work of learning everything Matt had to teach. For the first in a long time, she was relaxed and not feeling the stress of being in command.

SCIENCE HELPS A WHALE

Jason was aboard the Sadie Princess doing volunteer work for the Marine Education Research Society when he got a radio call from the Port Hardy Coast Guard Station.

"Sadie Princess, this is Port Hardy Coast Guard Station. Do you copy?"

"This is the Sadie Princess. I copy, over."

"Jason, this is Commander Brient. I wonder if you have time to check on some humpbacks near the entrance to the harbor? We have received reports that one of the whales seems to be in distress, over."

"Commander, send me the coordinates of the last sighting. I am close to the harbor entrance. I will find the whales and be in touch, over."

Once Jason received the coordinates of the last known whale location, he programmed his navigation system to plot a course to the site. Within thirty minutes he spotted three whales. There was something very wrong. By law, Jason was prohibited from approaching closer than one-hundred meters of the whales. From a distance, it looked like there were three whales, one on the left and one on the right of the center whale. The two outside whales were using their bodies to guide the whale in the middle. It appeared the center whale could not maintain a straight line while swimming.

Jason had never seen anything like this.

"Argonaut, I need your help. There are three whales near the harbor entrance. One whale is hurt or sick. Can you reach out to the them and ask if there is anything we can do to for them?" Jason asked.

Argonaut expanded his senses until he located the three whales swimming near the Sadie Princess.

"Hello, friends. My name is Argonaut the Inua humpback. My pod and I live in these waters. Are you hurt or sick? Can I help?" Argonaut said.

The three whales stopped swimming. They had never heard another whale speaking to them using telepathy.

"Where are you? Who are you? What are you?" the oldest male asked using his thoughts.

"I am a friend. I am not far from you. I can hear your thoughts and you can hear mine. One of my human friends saw you. He is close by in the boat you can hear. He thought one of you was hurt. I live near your current location. I and my human friend will do what we can to help," Argonaut said.

"I am called Kirki, my mate's name is Namani, and our son is called Valent. Our son is three seasons old. He was born with one good fin and one partial fin. With only one good fin, he is unable to swim in a straight line. He can dive and search for food, but not easily. We help him travel by staying on both sides of him. We were shunned by our pod because our son is different from other whales. We have wandered the oceans since our son was born. He would die if we left him alone," Kirki said.

"Swim towards the harbor. I and some of my family will meet you there. We live in a safe place with plenty of food. We can help care for Valent while you and Namani rest. You must be very tired," Argonaut said to Kirki.

While the three new whales swam towards the harbor, Argonaut reached out to Raven, Angel, Sitka, and his father. He asked them to join him in meeting the three whales that needed their help.

Knolhval said they would be there as quickly as they could. Argonaut swam to the harbor entrance. He saw the three whales. Argonaut immediately understood the difficulty. Valent's left pectoral fin was only half formed. His birth defect made it impossible for him to swim like other whales.

Argonaut slowly approached the family. Using whale sounds, he welcomed them. He asked Namani if he could take a turn helping to guide Valent. Namani was grateful for the chance to rest. She thanked the Inua.

Soon, Sitka, Angel, Raven, and Knolhval met the others swimming into the harbor. Argonaut introduced his matriarch and his family to the three newcomers.

Argonaut asked Kirki if Raven could take his place by Valent's other side so Kirki could rest. Kirki agreed to let Raven help his son. Kirki was exhausted and welcomed the chance to relax.

While the group was swimming south into the Johnstone Strait, Argonaut reached out to Jason.

"My friend, we need you again. This is a big favor to ask. In the group of whales you found there is one whale missing most of his left pectoral fin. The family has no one to help them care for their offspring. Will you meet us, look at the young whale, and see if you can help?" Argonaut asked.

Jason said, "I have to return to Port Hardy and fill the gas tanks with fuel. As soon as I fill the tanks on the Sadie Princess, I will leave the harbor and find you. I have my dive gear on board. When we meet, I will dive next to the whales so I can get a better look at the partial pectoral fin."

"This is something I have never seen before. I have no idea what to do," Argonaut said.

Jason arrived as soon as he could. He put on his scuba gear. He dove next to Valent. Argonaut explained to the three whales that the human was his friend. He told the whales that Jason might be able to help Valent.

Jason approached the whales slowly. He swam around Valent as the new whales watched him carefully.

Argonaut said, "What do you think? Is there anything that can be done for Valent? His family is exhausted from caring for him. They need food and rest. My pod will do what we can but we need to find a permanent fix for the young whale."

Jason had an idea. He explained his suggestion to Argonaut. Jason went back aboard Sadie Princess. He called his old friend, Dr. Skip Foster, the famous marine veterinarian from Vancouver.

"Hi, Skip. A humpback whale that just arrived in the strait has a unique problem. I have an idea of how to help the whale. I would like to get your opinion," Jason told his friend.

"You always have interesting problems. Tell me what you have in mind," Foster said.

Jason explained the situation with Valent's birth defect and told Foster his idea.

"That may be the craziest idea I have ever heard you utter. You have had several crazy schemes but even for you, this in unusual. Your suggestion has never been done on this scale before. It could cost hundreds of thousands of dollars. It will require unique equipment and experimental materials. It might take several weeks to pull this off, if it is even possible," said Foster.

"If I find the funding, can you arrange for the equipment and materials?" Jason asked.

"On one condition. I get to write this up for the Canadian Veterinarian Journal," Foster replied.

"Deal. I will start by securing the funding. You work on finding the equipment, supplies, and materials. I will ask Commander Brient to arrange for a ship, with cranes, to lift Valent onto the deck of the Canadian Coast Guard ship where you can examine the whale. The work can be done while the ship is at anchor," Jason said with excitement in his voice.

Jason called Wild Bill. He explained the problem and his idea of how to help Valent. Jason told Wild Bill he desperately wanted his plan to work so they could improve the quality of Valent's life. Will Bill said he would ask Commander Brient to have a ship and a large crane vessel available when the equipment and supplies were ready. Jim DeFord said he would ask the British Columbia Ferry line to bring the equipment to the Coast Guard ship when everything was in place.

Jason's next call was to Jill White Feather. He explained his plan. He told her they needed approximately two-hundred-thousand dollars to rent the equipment needed to save the whale. Jill said she would call Premier Guyaen and ask for his help. It would be a chance for Canada to show the rest of the world that the country was serious about saving earth and all its creatures.

The Premier agreed to help with Jill's request. Guyaen ordered the British Columbia Ferry company and the Coast Guard to cooperate with implementing Jason's plan.

Jason reached out to Argonaut. He explained his idea to the Inua.

"We are going to perform a complete 360-degree scan of Valent's left pectoral fin. With that scan and some computer modeling we are going to build a prothesis for Valent's left fin. A large-scale 3D printer will print a full-size pectoral fin prosthesis cover. The prosthesis will be attached, using a vest, to Valent's partial left pectoral fin. The vest will go over his right fin, circle his body like a glove, and keep the prosthesis in place over his left fin. If we are lucky, Valent may be able to lead a normal life. It will take several days to get the equipment here from Vancouver. The government will pay for some of the expenses. Can you keep Valent safe until we are ready to perform this procedure?" Jason asked.

Argonaut told Jason his pod would help Valent swim. The pod would drive bait fish to Valent so he could easily feed until it was time for the procedure.

Wild Bill and Commander Brient arranged for a crane vessel and a Coast Guard ship to be on standby. Dr. Foster rented a large portable scanner. The device was loaded aboard a BC Ferry for the trip to Port Hardy. Once in Port Hardy the scanner would be transferred to the Coast Guard ship. When the scan was completed, the results would be sent to a 3D print operation in Vancouver where the pectoral fin cover would be printed.

Dr. Foster and his team of nurses, prosthetic specialists, and animal orthopedic experts would meet Jason in Port Hardy once the scanner was in place.

Matt Hawk knew someone who could help raise funds. Wild Bill's daughter Elena Mendenhall lived in Vancouver. She was an avid animal rights activist. Elena was a world-famous supporter of animal adoptions and a successful real estate property manager. She was active in many social causes. She was also an internet influencer who had over one-hundred-thousand followers.

Matt called Elena.

"Hi. It's Matt. How are you?" he asked.

"Things are going great. Real estate market is strong. We are working hard on animal adoptions in the Vancouver area," she replied.

"I have a project I think you may want to be involved in. There is a young whale, Valent, who recently appeared in the northern end of Johnstone Strait. He has a birth defect. Most of his left pectoral fin is missing. Our goal is to have a prosthetic 3D fin produced and fitted for Valent. The new prosthesis would be held on by a vest that wraps around his body. The government will have a Coast Guard ship and crane vessel available for the procedure. We need about two-hundred-fifty-thousand dollars to pay for the scanner rental; print the fin cover; design and construct the internal skeleton and have it fitted. The vest will slip over his right pectoral fin then around his body to hold the new printed fin in place on his left side. I was hoping you would set up a Go Fund Me page to help raise enough money to save the young humpback. He has no quality of life. His parents struggle each day to keep him alive," Matt explained.

"I would love to help. Do you have any pictures of the whale? If so, send them to me. I will set up the website and start soliciting donations. We need a not-for- profit entity to accept the donations so they will be tax-deductible," Elena told Matt.

"MERS has agreed to be the agency of record for handling the funds. They are a not-for-profit. I will give you the bank account information so donors can make contributions directly to the Save Valent the Humpback account. I will email you some pictures of Valent right away," Matt said.

Elena went to work. Within the first twelve hours the Go Fund Me effort had raised over one-hundred-thousand dollars to save Valent.

Dr. Foster had the scanning equipment in transit to Port Hardy. Commander Brient arranged for the equipment to be loaded aboard the Canadian Coast Guard ship Teleost. The ship was a fisheries research vessel currently doing studies near the northern end of Vancouver Island. The CCGS Teleost is over two-hundred feet long. The deck of the Teleost is large enough to hold Valent while he is scanned for the design of his 3D printed fin cover. The CCGS Teleost just finished a major retrofit and was on its first Pacific Ocean based research trip.

Once the CCGS Teleost and scanner were in place, Jason asked Argonaut to help guide Valent to the ship docked in the strait not far from Port Hardy.

Dr. Foster wondered how they were going to keep a fifty-thousand-pound whale calm, still, and motionless while the scan was being done. Dr. Foster knew Jason was some sort of a whale whisperer but this was an extraordinary event. Dr. Foster did not want to use anesthesia medicine on Valent unless it was absolutely necessary.

Argonaut explained to Valent and his parents what would happen. The humans were going to lift Valent on to the ship. The people would use a machine to take pictures of Valent. Once the pictures were completed, the humans would put Valent back into the water.

"When my mate, Angel, was kidnapped, humans helped save her. Once she returned to our sanctuary, they lifted her from the pirate ship safely into the water. They will be very careful with Valent. The humans have a plan to build a new fin for Valent. The new fin will allow him to swim freely. Hopefully, if all goes well, he will not need to be guided by other whales. I trust my friends to take good care of Valent," said the Inua.

As Argonaut, Kirki, Namani and Valent swam to the CCGS Teleost, Jason told Argonaut to have Valent just relax. Divers from the ship would put carrying straps around the young humpback. The massive cranes on the nearby crane ship would lift the patient to the deck of the CCGS Teleost.

Aboard the ship were Dr. Foster and Dr. Nancy Mendenhall, the head of veterinarian orthopedics at the University of Canada in Vancouver. Dr. Mendenhall was the wife of Wild Bill Mendenhall and the mother of Elena and Marisa. Marisa was the general surgeon who saved the life of Commander Bruce Brient after he was shot protecting a Spirit Bear from hunters.

Argonaut used his Inua powers to enter the minds of the two doctors, the technicians, and ship crew members. He removed their worry about keeping Valent calm during the scan.

As Valent was lifted aboard ship, Kirki and Namani swam nervously close by. They called out using whale sound so their son could hear them. Valent remained calm as he was carefully laid on the deck of the CCGS Teleost. Valent believed in the Inua and his human friends. The young whale hoped the humans would help him. He was tired of being a burden to his parents. He wanted to swim like other whales.

"Skip, this is going to be difficult. We have to design a fin that can help guide a fifty-thousand-pound whale, survive breaching, deep water dives, cold temperatures, and not need replacement for many years. We cannot just slip the new fin over the stub of a fin that is there now. We need a way to keep the new fin in place. I have an idea of what we can do. We can 3D print a vest and slip it over the whale's right fin. A new left fin would be built into the vest. We could slip the apparatus over his stub and keep it in place. I have done this with dolphins," Dr. Mendenhall said.

"A dolphin's fin is very small compared to a humpback's pectoral fin. The sheer weight of the fin and the force of the whale's movements seems to make it impossible to design an object that will work," said Dr. Foster.

The scanner was on a large platform that enabled the technicians to scan every inch of Valent's body. Dr. Mendenhall supervised the scans. She reviewed the images. When she was satisfied, the images were sent to the 3D printer company in Vancouver for printing the vest cover. A second set of the images was sent to the Boeing aircraft manufacturing company in the United

States to be used in designing the interior of the prosthetic.

Dr. Mendenhall used her computer tablet to find a link to the Boeing aircraft company website. She clicked on a link to a video she asked Dr. Foster to watch.

The Boeing video showed a new type of airplane wing designed by the airplane manufacturer. The internal structure is made of titanium. The material is a very strong but light weight metal. The metal is then covered with hundreds of layers of a new substance called braeon. Braeon, according to its designers, is the world's most adaptable and strongest material.

"Boeing is interested in trying out the design process using our whale as a test subject. They have agreed to build the fin skeleton based on our 3D scans. Once the fin internal structure is finished, we will test fit it to the whale. Once we are sure of the fit, the 3D printer company will produce the cover made of polyactide (PLA). The polymer is heat and cold resistant. The fin and vest should last for decades, even with the stress of the whale breaching and diving. Airplane wings can last for many years under incredible stress. Boeing will develop the inner skeleton and coat it with many layers of braeon at their cost," said Dr. Mendenhall.

Jason was listening to the exchange and so was Argonaut. The Inua explained what the humans were saying to Valent and his family.

Valent was staying very calm while the multiple scans were completed. Once the technicians were finished, the crane lifted Valent slowly back into the water. He, Argonaut, Namani, and Kirki swam back towards Orca Lab. Sitka and the rest of the pod were waiting their return.

Elena Mendenhall called Jason.

"Hi. Have you looked at the MERS Go Fund Me Account for Valent recently?" she asked.

Jason replied," We have been busy with Valent. Do you have good news?"

"Our original goal was two-hundred-fifty thousand dollars for Valent's procedure. So far, we have raised over one-million dollars," she said.

"Wow. That's incredible. We can fund the entire procedure and use the remainder of the money to help other creatures in need. You did a great job," Jason said.

"The pictures of Valent's birth defect and his story are so moving. It encouraged many people who want to help," Elena said.

"Thank you for all your work. Maybe when the fin is attached you can make a trip to Telegraph Cove to meet Valent and his family," Jason told his friend.

Elena told Jason she would love to visit the whales.

The Boeing company builds giant 777 planes at the rate of five a month. It took the airplane manufacturer four days to design and build the pectoral fin skeleton. The fin inner structure of titanium and braeon was sent by ferry to Port Hardy then transferred to the CCGS Teleost.

Valent was once again lifted aboard the CCGS Teleost. Argonaut used his Inua powers one more time to stop people from wondering how they kept the whale so tranquil without anesthetics.

Dr. Mendenhall and Dr. Foster worked with technicians to check the fit of the skeleton. With some minor adjustments they were satisfied the skeleton was ready for the 3D cover.

The printing company printed the prosthesis cover in forty-eight hours. The cover was shipped airfreight to Port Hardy. Once the cover was aboard the CCGS Teleost it was fitted, with the help from the ship's sailors, over the prosthesis. The vest slid over the right fin, the middle of Valent's body, and snuggly over his new left fin skeleton. The vest had been printed using braeon. It was stronger than traditional airplane wing skin and much more flexible. The outer skin was black and it blended perfectly with the vest color and Valent's own skin color. He would not have to be ashamed of his deformity any longer.

Once the new fin and vest were in place, Valent was lifted back into the calm waters of the Johnstone Strait. Argonaut told Valent to stay very still until he could float away from the ship. Valent moved his fluke and swam in a straight line. He then slowly did a large left-hand turn on top of the water using his pectoral fins. Next, he dove and did a small breach. Over the next several days, Valent did more and more dramatic movements. He dove and breached with more force and energy. He had soon mastered maneuvering using his new pectoral fin. For the first time in his life, Valent was able to move in every direction. His parents would no longer need to guide his every move.

Using their scuba gear, Jason and Matt dove next to Valent. They thoroughly inspected the vest and prosthetic fin. Everything looked perfect.

"Looks fine from here," Jason said.

"I agree. This is an engineering marvel," Matt exclaimed.

Valent told Argonaut the fin fit well and he had no discomfort.

Dr. Mendenhall told Dr. Foster, "I want to see him in thirty days for a follow-up visit. Let me know if there are any problems."

The event was carried live on Canadian television and on the National Geographic channel. Photographers from many news outlets were present to photograph Valent.

This was the largest prosthesis ever designed.

Premier Guyaen called Dr. Foster and Dr. Mendenhall to congratulate them on the successful procedure.

"Donors, you, Boeing, the CCGS Teleost crew, technicians, and the 3D printer company did the hard work. I hope you get a chance to visit and see Valent in person," Dr. Foster told the Premier.

"I will make a point to visit Telegraph Cove, the next time I am in the Vancouver area," said the Premier.

Valent, Namani, and Kirki all thanked Argonaut and his pod for helping Valent.

Argonaut explained to the three whales that they were welcome to stay and be part of Sitka's pod. Valent had an appointment in thirty days to be examined by the doctors. It made sense for them to stay near Telegraph Cove where the whales were safe and there was plenty of food.

"Why did you help me? I was different. I was not like other whales. I was weak and ugly. I was ashamed of the way I looked. We were driven from our pod because I was deformed. You took me and my family under your protection. You and your friends helped me get a new fin. I do not understand why you did all that for a stranger," Valent said.

"We are all part of the same world. No matter how we look, where we come from, how we sound, or how different we are. Each of us owes it to others to be kind and caring. I have learned that all creatures have the capacity to care. Being different does not make us bad," the Inua said.

"I will try to be the best whale I can be. If there is an opportunity to help other creatures, I will do my best. I will always remember what you have taught me," Valent replied.

He used his new left pectoral fin to reach out and touch Argonaut, as a sign of affection. Argonaut, the great Inua, was moved. There was a small tear of joy in the great Inua's eye.

Valent swam to join his parents and the Sitka pod. For the first time in his life, Valent did not need the help of others to swim.

VALENT WITH NEW PROSTHETIC PECTORAL FIN

IT'S PARTY TIME

Canada's National Indigenous Peoples Day, formerly called National Aboriginal Day, is annually held on June 21 to celebrate the unique heritage, diverse cultures, and outstanding achievements of the country's First Nation peoples.

The tribes living in the Vancouver Island area decided to hold their second annual First Nations Festival on the island of Klemtu on June 21st.

There would be dancing, singing, contests, games, and a silent auction. The money raised would benefit the Marine Education Research Society, Orca Lab, and Project HOPE.

After the tremendous publicity surrounding the televised operation to devise and attach the prothesis to Valent, there was more interest than usual in the events near Vancouver Island from people around the world.

A silent auction with on-line, phone, and in person bidding was scheduled for the day of the festival.

Donated items included a dinner for four at La Terraza del Casino de Vancouver. It is regarded as the best Spanish restaurant in all of Canada. It is owned and operated by Terie DeFord. Terie is the wife of Captain Jim DeFord. She is a graduate of Le Cordon Bleu in Paris, the famous cooking school. Terie trained at some of the finest restaurants in the world. She is the head chef at La Terraza. The restaurant is so renowned the wait time for reservations is often more than six months.

For the auction, Jason had framed pictures of Argonaut breaching, T-Rex and Little Rex simultaneously tail slapping, and a picture of a pacific white-sided dolphin doing a complete flip out of the water.

Matt and General Choate (USAF Retired) donated a full-day cruise for a party of ten on the Orcella 2 to see the sites around Telegraph Cove.

Wild Bill Mendenhall donated two half-day helicopter rides for two people. The flights would take the high bidders around the rain forest territory looking for Spirit Bears and other wildlife in the Johnstone Strait area.

Captain Jim DeFord offered an evening cruise for six, meals and beverages included, aboard his boat Hercules. His wife Terie would cook a special Spanish themed meal for guests on the cruise.

Local First Nation artisans offered paintings, moccasins, large and small totem carvings, plus much more for sale in the auction.

The games began at nine in the morning. There were foot races, spear-throwing contests, rowing competitions, dancing, and games for the children.

Over eight-hundred people attended the event. The lunch-time meal included salmon, crab, halibut, corn, and squash biscuits. Indian pudding was the dessert. This traditional dish, first made in the eastern parts of North America, is rich in both history and flavor. It's made by combining cornmeal and milk with molasses. It's one of the first truly American recipes.

Dance competitions among the various tribes were spirited.

As the day was ending, Chief White Feather introduced his daughter, Jill, who made the closing announcements.

"Today was a wonderful day. We enjoyed ourselves. We are surrounded by our family and friends. The auction raised over sixty-thousand dollars for MERS, Orca Lab, and Project HOPE. I received a phone call this morning that I want to share with you. We, the six directors of Project HOPE, have been invited to speak to the United Nations General Assembly next month. Our people are making a difference in the world. Thank you for coming to our island today. May the Great Spirits keep you safe," Jill said.

Jill received a standing ovation from the crowd.

As the different families started to go home, by boat or specially charted ferries, Jill heard from her Inua friend.

"I have been listening to you and your friends as you work so hard to help save the world. For someone so young, you are strong and brave. I am proud to know you," Argonaut said.

"We are doing the best we can. You may be our biggest ally, both in size and force of personality. Your voice had a huge impact on Canadian legislators. In a few weeks you and Project HOPE will be speaking to members of the United Nations, one of the most important groups in the world. It is critical that we not fail. Failure means disaster for you, your family, and all creatures of the earth," Jill told Argonaut.

"There is no one I trust more. Together we will do the best we can to have everyone work together to help us. We are few but our voices are strong. Stay well my young Princess Warrior," Argonaut told Jill.

She was moved to be called a Princess Warrior by one of the greatest beings on earth. It made her very proud to be friends with the Inua Argonaut.

KITASOO VISIT THE UNITED NATIONS

The current Secretary General of the United Nations (UN) is Dr. L. K. Rothman of Sweden. He is the former Prime Minister of Sweden. Rothman is best known for winning the Nobel Peace Prize for negotiating a truce in 2021 between the Palestinians and Israelis. His efforts led to a treaty settling differences that were ongoing for many generations between two ancient civilizations.

Dr. Rothman called Jill White Feather in early June. He invited her and the other Project HOPE directors to address the UN General Assembly on July 4th of this year. International Day of Cooperatives is celebrated by the UN every year on July 4th. Cooperatives for Climate Action was chosen as the theme for this year's celebration of cooperation among UN member countries.

No one on earth will escape the devastation from disasters, if climate change is not brought under control. Since Project HOPE has chapters in virtually every country of the world, it seemed appropriate for the young Kitasoo to be the speakers at this year's annual UN event.

"Miss White Feather, thank you for agreeing to be with us at the UN in New York on July 4th. I listened with great interest to your address to the Canadian legislators. I also have read numerous accounts of the message sent to the legislators by the Inua. I hope your Inua friend speaks to the members of the UN General Assembly. The International Day of Cooperatives this year has a focus on climate change. Your group is doing extraordinary work. We are anxious to meet you in person," said Secretary General Rothman.

"Thank you, Mr. Secretary General, for the opportunity to speak to the UN. We are excited for the chance to visit with you and representatives of so many different countries from around the world. The Inua is aware of the event and has promised to visit with those gathered in New York," Jill replied.

Secretary General Rothman told Jill about the ancient Norse God Tyr. The ancient Tyr, at one time was a very important part of the Norse mythology. He was often thought to be an upholder of justice and law. Tyr made a great personal sacrifice to protect others from the evil Fenrir.

The Secretary General asked if Jill knew the

story of the ancient wolf Fenrir. Jill told Secretary General Rothman she had not heard the Fenrir myth.

Rothman explained that in Norse legend, mythical gods raised the vicious wolf Fenrir. They wanted to keep him under their control and prevent him from wreaking havoc throughout the world. He grew at an astonishingly fast pace. Eventually, the troubled gods decided to confine Fenrir with chains. Their first two attempts at chaining the mythical wolf were unsuccessful. Fenrir easily broke his chains. The gods convinced Fenrir that it was only a game, a test of his strength. Finally, the gods had the dwarves forge the strongest chain ever built. The magical chain was designed to fool Fenrir. The chain appeared light and soft to the touch. The gods presented Fenrir with this third chain. By this time, he was very suspicious of the gods and their chains. He refused to be bound with the new chain unless one of the gods would stick his or her hand in Fenrir's mouth as a pledge of good faith. Only Tyr was brave enough to do this, knowing it would mean the loss of his hand. He gave much of himself to save the world.

"Your Inua friend seems much like the Norse Tyr of legend. He appears to be a creature fighting for justice for all creatures on this planet. He is putting his life at risk for all of us as Tyr did with the wolf Fenrir. I often think of pollution and climate change as modern-day examples of Fenrir," said Secretary General Rothman.

Jill explained the Inua she knew did many small and great things to protect not only his kind but many other creatures. The Inua that Jill knew often put the lives and safety of others first, even if it might cost him his life.

"You are right in comparing the Inua to the ancient mythical Tyr. I know of no creature that is more fair, honest, kind, and willing to sacrifice his life for others than the Inua. If his identity is revealed it will likely mean death for, he and his family," Jill said.

"Someday, when I am retired from the UN, I would like to visit Klemtu, the great Spirit Bear Lodge, and get to know the beautiful land where you live," said Rothman.

"My people would be honored to have such a famous and respected world leader visit our island. We will see you soon in New York," Jill told the Secretary General.

On July 2nd, Jill and her friends flew from Vancouver to New York City. Upon arriving at LaGuardia airport, the group took a shuttle to the

New York Millennium Hilton at One UN Plaza.

On July 3rd the UN arranged for a day of sightseeing for the young Kitasoo. They visited Times Square, World Trade Center memorial site, Museum of Modern Art, Metropolitan Museum, Empire State Building and Statute of Liberty. It was a long and exciting day. The Kitasoo were especially moved by the World Trade Center memorial fountain. So many had died needlessly. The Kitasoo knew that many others would die if they failed in their efforts to help save earth.

That evening the Secretary General hosted a dinner in honor of the Project HOPE directors. Ambassadors from over forty countries met to greet and speak with the Project HOPE representatives. The event lasted until midnight. By the time the group were finally settled in their rooms, they were exhausted.

At 10 AM on July 4th, the Kitasoo were escorted to the dais of the UN General Assembly hall. The six Project HOPE directors stood before the members of the UN General Assembly. As they were introduced, they were greeted by a standing ovation. It was at that moment, perhaps for the first time, the six young individuals from the small island of Klemtu knew they were making a difference.

Mary Raven was chosen to speak for the group. As she faced the gathered assembly, she knew this was the most important moment of her young life.

"Mr. Secretary, ambassadors and everyone here in this famous hall, on behalf of my fellow directors, I thank you for the great honor and privilege of speaking to your today. At no time in the history of our planet has it been more important for us to coordinate our efforts to save earth. Pollution is rampant. Water levels are rising around the globe. Species extinctions are accelerating. Poverty is becoming even more common as earth's population grows at an alarming rate.

You represent powerful voices for change. You are respected in your countries. Your opinions matter. We cannot act individually or even as one isolated country. We need to act in cooperation as a universal voice. Laws need to change. Scientists must be heard. Profits cannot be the sole purpose of corporate existence.

We all know the facts. We know there are many possible ways to help prevent the destruction of earth. I would like you to hear from one particularly strong and unique voice. The words you are about to hear hopefully will motivate you to action," said Mary.

Argonaut reached across the entire continent of North America into the mind of every individual assembled in the main hall of the UN.

"Friends, I am the Inua of whom you may have heard. You have listened to the words of my young Kitasoo friends. My place in this world is becoming too warm, too dirty, and too polluted. I see a future where my kind will not survive. Even I an Inua, cannot stop the dangers. Only you, and those in power where you live, can prevent the destruction of our world. What more warning does humanity need? You have seen fires, hurricanes, typhoons, floods, red tides, massive bird kills, and much more. It may already be too late. If you do not try then there is no future for the young people standing before you. Your descendants are doomed to suffer unless you enact the changes put forth by Project HOPE. On this special day of cooperation, please rise and stand united for change. People have brought earth to this crisis and only strong people of character like you can lead us from the brink of total annihilation of all creatures on this planet. I love my family as you love yours. I want to see my children, their children, and many future generations flourish. Please, act now," said Argonaut.

Led by Secretary General Rothman, the group

stood. The ambassadors applauded the Inua and the Project HOPE directors.

Once the ovation had subsided, Secretary General Rothman gave each of the six Kitasoo a Champion of the Earth Award. This is the highest civilian award given by the UN for global impact on environmental causes.

Jill thanked the assembly for the honor and promised to continue the fight for Project HOPE.

Early the next day, the group flew first to Vancouver and then to Port Hardy. Jim DeFord took the Project HOPE directors home to Klemtu aboard his ship, Hercules.

While on the Hercules traveling to Klemtu from Port Hardy, Jill reached out to Argonaut.

"You did very well my great Inua friend. Your voice is powerful, moving, and impactful. You and Project HOPE make a great team," Jill said,

"I am pleased that together we may change the world. I will do all I can to help, my dear great young Princess Warrior," Argonaut replied.

MARY RAVEN ADDRESSES THE UNITED NATIONS

GUARDIAN SAVES A BEAR FAMILY

Guardian was enjoying a lone swim north of the harbor of Vancouver Island. Sometimes it is nice to just relax and be by yourself. Being with the pod has many advantages but all creatures crave a little solitude on occasion. Guardian was enjoying a little "me time".

As Guardian was swimming about a mile south of Haida Gwaii he saw a strange sight. Three black bears were floating out to sea on a large log. The log was moving with the easterly wind and the outgoing tide. The humpback knew bears could swim but they were too far from shore to swim to safety.

It looked to be a mother bear with two young cubs. Guardian did not think the cubs would be able to make the long swim back to shore. How had the bears floated so far from land? The tide was swift. If someone did not help, the bears would soon be lost at sea.

Guardian used whale sounds to call out for

Matt on the Orcella 2. Matt heard the sounds. He knew it was one of the Sitka pod. Matt and Angie were testing new hydrophones and speakers before their next visitor cruise. Matt was reluctant to use the Wet PC translation software because Angie Choate was not one of the people who knew about the whales' ability to communicate.

Matt reached out to Argonaut and asked if the Inua thought it would be acceptable to share his secret with Angie, his new first mate.

"The lady who flew the plane that helped Angel can be trusted. Tell her what you must. Save the bears," said Argonaut.

Matt put the hydrophones over the side of the boat. Using the hydrophones, he recorded the sounds made by Guardian. The software translated the whale sounds that Guardian made into English. Matt understood there were three bears in danger. He started the boat. He steered the Orcella 2 towards Guardian's location near Haida Gwaii.

"Where are we going?" Angie asked.

Matt replied, "The best way to explain, is to just show you."

Soon the Orcella 2 found Guardian and the three bears.

Matt typed into the computer and said to Guardian, "We will tie a rope to the wood. We will pull the bears back to shore."

Angie watched in fascination as Matt typed into the computer and the words were translated into humpback sounds broadcast to Guardian via underwater speakers.

Matt used a grappling hook to carefully attach a rope to the log to which the bears were clinging. He slowly started the Orcella 2 towards Haida Gwaii pulling the log and the bears. Within two hours the log was close to shore. The mother bear and her cubs jumped off. The three exhausted bears swam to shore. As the bears reached land, the mother turned and looked at the Orcella 2. She stood on her hind legs and growled while waving her two front paws. She could not speak to Matt but he knew what the mother was trying to say. The mother bear was clearly thankful to the humans who had saved her family.

The exhausted bears slowly made their way into the nearby woods.

Guardian had been spyhopping. Once he was certain the bears were safe, the humpback thanked Matt for his help.

Angie tapped Matt on the shoulder and said, "Can you explain what just happened? It looked as if you were talking to a whale and that the whale was talking to you."

"It's a long story. Several years ago, Jason was working for the Coast Guard using the Wet PC Underwater computer. He met Argonaut, a large humpback. They accidentally discovered they could communicate using the computer. Argonaut made whale sounds and Jason recorded them on the computer. Jason used flash cards to develop a vocabulary for Argonaut so they could easily speak to each other. Soon they were talking to one another using the underwater computer. Over time, Argonaut, as he grew into his full Inua talents, could communicate using just his thoughts. Jason and Argonaut did not need the Wet PC. All the other whales in Sitka's pod have learned to respond to the sounds from the Wet PC and to communicate with us," Matt said.

Matt asked his first mate if she knew what an Inua was?

"If memory serves me correctly, an Inua is sort of a combination shaman, angel, and mystic. Is that about right?" she asked.

Matt smiled and said, "Argonaut is all that and much more."

Angie looked at Matt with astonishment. "Whales can talk to people and people can talk to whales? Are you kidding me?" she asked.

Matt looked at Angie and said, "It gets even

better. Have you heard of Argonaut before now?"

"Sure. He used to live here but moved to Alaska," Angie said.

"Nope. That is just a story we told everyone to help keep Argonaut's identity a secret. Argonaut is the famous Inua you have read about. Sort of a magical whale that can communicate using telepathy. He can see into the future. He has the ability to control others with his mind. His is the voice that spoke to the Canadian legislators and the UN General Assembly. We put a cover over his tail so he could not be identified," Matt explained.

"Was he involved in the whale kidnapping and the destruction of the North Korean submarine? The whale who was kidnapped was named Angel, if I remember correctly," she said.

"Angel, the whale you helped save from the kidnappers, is Argonaut's mate," Matt said.

"Let's see if I have this straight. There is a magical whale that can use telepathy, foresee the future, and affect creatures with his mind. He is the Inua I have heard so much about and he is your friend?" she asked.

Matt nodded and reached out to Argonaut.

"Hey big fella. I think you may want to say hello to Angie before she throws me overboard. She thinks I'm crazy," Matt thought to Argonaut.

"Hello, Angie. I'm Argonaut the Inua. I never got a chance to thank you for helping to save my mate after she was taken from our home. I also know you helped destroy the underwater boat that was trying to harm us. Welcome to our home waters," Argonaut thought to Angie.

"Wow. I thought flying jets was a rush. This is the most incredible experience of my life. Do you know what I think anytime you want?" Angie asked.

The Inua responded, "Yes, I can see into your mind. I do not invade people's thoughts unless it is to save a life or prevent harm. I stay pretty busy helping creatures in our sanctuary. Matt has helped me many times. He and Jason saved my son from drowning in a net. Being an Inua is not something I asked for. It just happened one day. My powers have gotten stronger as I get older."

"Why did you have a cover put on your tail? Are you not proud of being an Inua and being known as Argonaut?" Angie asked.

"My being an Inua could lead to danger to me and my pod, if the secret were known by the wrong people. We would be hounded and perhaps even hunted. Only a few people know who I am. I trust you will not share my story with anyone," Argonaut said.

"I have a top-secret military grade department of defense clearance with the US government. I am trustworthy. I will honor your request. I must say, it is going to be interesting living and working in these waters with an Inua and a pod of whales that can talk to humans," the former general said.

"Life is never dull here. If you ever need help general, just reach out to me. My pod and I owe Jason, Matt, you, and many other humans our lives," Argonaut told Angie.

Matt taught Angie how to use the Wet PC to understand whale sounds and to call out to the whales. He explained how Guardian had called out for help with the stranded bears.

"Are there any more secrets about life in these straits you care to share?" she asked.

"I have spent most of my life on these waters. Even after all this time, I am constantly surprised and amazed. We never seem to get bored," Matt explained.

The two boaters started the engine on the Orcella 2. They began motoring back to Telegraph Cove.

Angie was deeply moved by what she had learned about the whales. If whales could talk maybe other creatures were more intelligent than humans thought. It was a lot to absorb. She began to understand even more about the attraction of the Vancouver straits to Matt and Jason. This really was a magical place.

THREE BEARS FLOATING OUT TO SEA

JASON FINISHES SCHOOL

For seven years, Jason has been studying for his Doctorate in Marine Biology. Finally, he submitted his dissertation for review by his supervising committee. He was preparing for his oral examinations at the University of Canada in Vancouver.

His dissertation topic was "Behaviors of Humpback Whales – A Study in Pod Dynamics of British Columbia's Cetaceans."

Jason had thousands of hours of video and audio recordings of the Sitka pod interfacing with each other, the orca, and dolphins. Jason's hypothesis was humpbacks were extraordinarily intelligent. Jason knew humpbacks could communicate effectively with each other and with other species.

His research spanned over twenty-five years in the waters of Vancouver Island. He had video footage of the humpbacks supporting Raven when he was trapped in the net. Jason had taped the non-violent confrontation as the humpbacks, orca, and dolphins faced the great white sharks. Much of what Jason knew could never be published without the danger of exposing Argonaut's Inua powers.

Recordings of whales singing with responses received from whales in the same pod proved the hypothesis that communication by sound was part of humpback behavior. Group feeding using cooperation and coordination had been verified. Tracing the matriarchal lineage of the Sitka pod proved there was a set structure to the society of some pods. Necropsies had proven the dangers to humpbacks from pollution.

The supervising doctoral committee was favorably impressed with Jason's dissertation and oral defense. He was awarded his Doctorate in Marine Biology.

As soon as the committee announced their decision, Jason called Matt.

"I made it. I am the newest Doctor of Marine Biology in Canada," Jason told his best human friend.

"Congratulations. I know how hard you have worked. It is a well-deserved distinction. See you when you get home," Matt told his friend.

As Jason's Pacifica Airlines flight from Vancouver was descending into Port Hardy airport, he saw a group of people standing near the terminal. They had balloons, signs, and were all waving at the plane.

At first Jason thought there must be someone famous on the plane. As soon as he entered the terminal, he saw Matt, Commander Mendenhall, Captain DeFord, the six Kitasoo Project Hope directors, and many other friends and neighbors.

"Wow. This is a surprise. How did you know I would pass the exam?" Jason asked.

Everyone laughed at such a silly question. They all started singing For He's A Jolly Good Fellow.

Matt gave Jason a gift from the group.

It was a carved wooden humpback breaching from the sea. It was a stunning piece. It had been carved by an award winning sculptor from New Bedford, Massachusetts.

Jason was overwhelmed. It was an incredible piece of art. It reminded him of the art that Raven had given him for saving Raven's life.

Jason thanked everyone. The group started a caravan to Telegraph Cove where Matt and Angie had planned a large party in Jason's honor.

There was singing, dancing, fireworks, and plenty of food and drink.

Finally, near midnight, everyone made their way home. It was just Matt, Angie, and Jason sitting on the deck of the Orcella 2. It was a full moon and the nighttime visibility was incredible.

"One of the best days of my life. Thank you for a great party," Jason said.

"We have one more little surprise for you. Take a look out in the strait. Right in front of us, just keep looking," Matt told his friend.

All at once, in perfect unison, thirty-five humpbacks breached. They breached together a second and finally a third time.

Argonaut reached out to Jason and said, "Never in the history of our kind have this many humpbacks breached at the same time. You have been a wonderful friend to me and our pod. We owe you much. We hope you like our small gift."

Jason had tears in his eyes. What he, Matt, and Angie had just witnessed was the first and only time anything like this had ever happened. The mutual respect and admiration between the whales and these humans were remarkable.

"Please tell your family that I am honored. I feel as much love for you and your pod as I do for anyone or anything else in the world. You have given me the perfect gift on a perfect day. I will never forget the magic and majesty of your breaches. Thank you, dear Inua friend," Jason said to Argonaut.

Argonaut told his pod what Jason had said. All

the whales were proud of what they had done. They slowly started swimming to deeper water. It had been a good day in the straits of Vancouver.

RED TIDE APPROACHES THE STRAITS

Jason was aboard the CCGS Risley doing whale location surveys. He was using a sophisticated video drone when he spotted a large discoloration in the water floating north from the coastal border with the United States.

Jason used the drone to take extended video footage of the floating red cloud. He sent the video recording to Dr. Beth Mallard, a friend in the marine research department at the University of Canada in Vancouver.

Jason called Dr. Mallard. "Hi, Beth. Did you receive the drone video I sent?"

"I did. This is a red tide bloom. I have never seen one this far north. I assume the warming water temperatures are making the blooms more likely in Canadian territory," she replied.

"If I remember my marine biology courses, red tide is a bloom of phytoplankton. In a bloom, a particular species of phytoplankton begins reproducing rapidly causing millions of cells in a gallon of water," Jason said.

"You are absolutely correct. The cells contain a pigment used to collect sunlight that is needed for organism nourishment and growth," Dr. Mallard explained.

Jason was worried the red tide bloom might be harmful to the fish and mammals of the Vancouver Island waters.

"Do we need to be concerned about the bloom affecting the wildlife of the area?" Jason asked the marine biologist.

"The bloom can last for days, weeks, or even months. It depends on the water temperature, winds, amount of sunlight, and the creatures that feed on the phytoplankton. Some blooms are harmless. Occasionally, the red tide is caused by harmful toxins and can be very dangerous to wildlife. Normally, the biggest danger is to shellfish like oysters and clams. There was a famous case in the 1940s in Florida where sea mammals ate a lot of zooplankton poisoned by a toxic bloom. That bloom cased a massive kill-off of sea mammals in the area," said Dr. Mallard.

"How do we know if this bloom is toxic or not?" Jason asked his friend.

Dr. Mallard said, "If you provide me a sample of water from the bloom, I can have our lab run a toxicity screen. How soon can you get me a sample?"

"Our ship will return to Port Hardy in three days. I can send you a sample by plane. You should have it in four days," Jason said.

"It will take about twenty-four hours to run the tox screen. We should know the answer about toxicity of the bloom within five days," Dr. Mallard explained to Jason.

"Let me know as soon as you can. I do not know if there is a way to keep wildlife away from the bloom. If it's toxic, we'll need to try and do something. Thank you," Jason said.

Argonaut had been listening to Jason speak with Dr. Mallard.

The Inua spoke to Jason using telepathy.

"Are we in danger from this floating color in the water?" Argonaut asked.

"We will not know for five days if the red water is dangerous to krill, salmon, or even larger animals like you," Jason told the Inua.

"What should we do to protect ourselves?" Argonaut asked.

"I think the best advice is for all the animals to feed far north of the red colored water. Feed far out to sea away from the bad water," Jason said.

Argonaut paused and said, "There are more humpbacks, salmon, krill, orca, dolphin, sea lions, and great whites in our home than stars in the sky. It will be impossible to move all wildlife from the sanctuary. Even my Inua power will never be enough to save all of us."

"What if you spoke to the leaders of the orca, dolphins, sea lions, and sharks. Ask them to help you drive the smaller fish from the straits. The larger fish might follow. The larger creatures will follow you and their leaders. Do you think that might work?" Jason replied.

"The salmon will not stop swimming to where they were born. If they go through the red water, they may be poisoned then the bears might get sick," said Argonaut.

Jason asked Argonaut if he could ask the bears to not eat fish for five days until the scientists studied the sample.

Argonaut shook his giant head and said, "Asking a bear not to eat fish is like asking a whale not to breathe. I will ask but I do not think I can stop all creatures from eating food that may come from the red water."

Jason told Argonaut they might get lucky and the bloom could be benign.

"All you can do is your best. The weather forecast is for storms next week. With strong winds and slightly cooler temperatures the red tide may disappear," Jason explained.

Argonaut called the pod together. He explained the potential danger of the red water. He reached out to the orca, dolphins, sharks, sea lions, eagles, and bears. He warned them of the possible poison from fish eaten from the red water.

"How long must we starve?" asked the eldest orca.

"I am not sure. My pod is going to swim out to sea. We will stay away from the red water. My human friend will know in five sunsets if the water is poisonous. If we stay away from the red water, we should be safe. Will you join us?" Argonaut asked the orca.

"We will swim with you. The powerful Inua had been kind to us and we trust him," the orca said.

Soon, the largest combined marine mammal and fish migration in history began from the Vancouver straits. Virtually every sea mammal in the area swam behind Sitka's pod. The animals swam about five miles out to sea. They drove as many bait fish as they could out to sea in front of the migration.

"We will take turns guarding ourselves from predators and large ships. I will listen carefully for word from my human friend about the red water. Hopefully, we will be able to go home soon," the

Inua told the multitude of animals.

In five days, a strong storm came through the area. Just as the red water was approaching the gathered mammals, Jason reached out to Argonaut.

"I received the report we have been waiting for. This time, the red water will not harm you or the fish you feed on. You can tell all the animals they can go back to the sanctuary. The bears can feed again," Jason said.

Argonaut explained the situation. He asked the orca, sharks, and dolphins to lead the vast group back to their homes. The humpbacks were the last to return to the sanctuary.

As the thousands of animals slowly returned to the waters of Vancouver Island, both Jason and Argonaut knew they had been lucky this red tide bloom was not toxic. If global warming was not controlled, the next red tide could be fatal to the animals.

MEMORY KEEPER STORIES ARE NEVER DONE

Argonaut sought out his matriarch, Sitka. He asked if she would tell him more stories from the legends passed down by memory keepers.

"Have you seen the bright lights that shine in the northern sky on some cooler evenings?" Sitka asked the Inua.

Argonaut said that he had seen them a few times. Knolhval had told his son that when he was living in the colder parts of the sea much to the north, these bright lights could be seen almost every night.

"One of the many stories of these bright lights comes from a land far to the east, where the sun appears each morning. The legend says that a famous god, called Odin, was revered by all people of his world. When Odin entered battle, he would pick the warriors who would die in the battle. The ones Odin had chosen would join him in the heavens, or Valhalla as these people called it.

Female warriors of this tribe were called the Valkyries. They were fierce fighters who wore bright armor. The legend says that the bright lights in the skies are reflections from the armor of the female Valkyrie warriors," Sitka told Argonaut.

Argonaut thought about Sitka's telling of the legend of Odin and the Valkyries. He realized there must be many battles, if the lights appear almost every night in the cold waters to the north. Argonaut began to understand that legends are often just stories. Many of the memory keeper stories may be fables and not facts.

"In another land, humans believe small animals, called Artic foxes, run across the sky so fast that their tails hit snow. The snow is then swept into the sky making the bright lights," Sitka explained.

"I have never seen anything except birds in the sky," Argonaut replied.

"I am just repeating the stories I have heard all my life. It is like the legend of the Inua. Until you grew into your powers I had never seen or heard an Inua speak, now I have one living with me in my pod. You are real. Maybe Odin, the Valkyries, or the Artic foxes making bright lights are real," Sitka said.

"Are there more stories about animals of the sea like us?" Argonaut asked his matriarch.

"Many of the stories about sea creatures are not happy ones. The memory keepers knew that many humans were afraid of the water. It was not natural for people to live in water like it is for us. There are many frightening stories of creatures from many different seas," Sitka replied.

"Tell me about some of these monsters," Argonaut said.

Sitka shared several tales of ancient sea creatures. "There are stories of a horse that lived near water. The horse was called Backahasten. This mysterious horse would appear when it was foggy and lure humans to ride on her back. Once a human was on the horse they could not get off. The horse would dive into the water. Once in the water, the humans would drown.

"Far to the west, where the sun disappears each day, there are legends of the Dragon Kings. There were four kings. One for the seas in the north, south, east, and west. These kings could change their shapes. They lived in palaces guarded by fierce sea creatures.

"Kraken is said to be a sea monster that lives deep in the sea. The monster rises from time to time to attack human ships and destroy people on the boats."

The two whales swam together going south towards Orca Lab. The water was calm. The sun was beginning to set in the west.

"Do the memory keepers have legends about the stars, sun, and moon?" Argonaut asked.

"There are many stories of the stars, sun, and moon. One of my favorites about the sun involves your old friend, the Inua Raven Hrafn. Once upon a time, in the beginning, there was no sun. The world was not very light. The great spirit kept the sun for himself in a box high in the sky. One day, Hrafn went through a hole in the sky and stole the box from the great spirit. Hrafn opened the box and the sun is now in the sky for all time," Sitka told Argonaut.

"Are there more stories from the memory keepers that you will share with me?" Argonaut asked.

"Our kind have been in the waters of the world since the beginning. We have seen many things. Of course, I will share more stories with you. It is late and I am tired. I am not a young whale anymore. I need my rest. Talking to an Inua is very challenging.

You are so smart, strong, young, energetic, and your mind so quick that you wear me out. You make me very happy, my brave Inua. I am proud you are part of our pod. I have never once been disappointed in you. I think one day soon, you will become part of many legends for the memory keepers to learn about. I think stories of Argonaut will be told for all time," Sitka told Argonaut.

Argonaut nodded as he and his matriarch rejoined the pod. The Inua hoped the legends of his life would be good memories for future memory keepers to share.

Argonaut felt a sudden coldness and he shuddered. The water was warm and he had never shuddered like this before. He did not feel sick. It was as if a dark spirit had just passed through him. Argonaut was fearful of what the future held for him.

Argonaut knew that his potential death was very close at hand.

SITKA LEADS A QUEST

Sitka called Angel, Rainbow, Biggsy, and Mother Biggsy to join her early one morning in August. The water was still warm in the northern Vancouver area. Food was plentiful. There was peace and tranquility in the sanctuary. The matriarch told the four female whales who had joined her, that it was time for them to make their quest to the ancient whale burial grounds. None of the other four had ever made the trip. It was important for the traditional quest to be made by females as well as males. In the culture of whales both males and females have equal status.

"When do we start?" Angel asked.

Sitka looked at her four friends and said, "We start now. I have spoken to the others in the pod and told them we are leaving. We may be gone for many days depending on how long it takes to spot the animals we must find."

Rainbow looked at Angel and asked, "Why didn't you make the quest when you were my age?"

"I was an orphan. My parents were both

tangled in fishing nets and died. Sitka's pod adopted me. I am long overdue for this journey. I am excited to be going with you, Biggsy, Sitka, and Mother Biggsy," Angel replied.

Sitka led the group north from Telegraph Cove towards the home of the Spirit Bears. They easily spotted a salmon. The quest group soon saw eagles that were fishing. Orca pods were feasting on the salmon swimming to their spawning grounds. The five whales saw ravens sitting high in the trees of Klemtu Island.

Sitka explained to the others about totems. The humpbacks are represented by the giant logs that are used to make the totems. The Spirit Bear is so sacred and secret that it is not shown on the totem, but is known to all those who live in these waters. The raven, salmon, orca, and black bears are the usual faces on a totem.

Biggsy asked Sitka about the Spirit Bear. "Does the white bear have magical powers like Argonaut?" she asked.

Sitka thought for a moment and said, "Being a different color does not make you magical. The Spirit Bear is sacred to the humans who live in this area because it is so rare. Only a few white bears live in these forests. Often, we fear what is different. Part of this quest is to show humpback whales that being different is not a bad thing. The whale, Valent, who received a new fin with Argonaut's assistance and human help was different, but he was never a bad whale. The Spirit Bears are honored, not because of their magical powers, but because they are so rare. Humans are different than we are. Often, we do not understand why they do things. I sometimes think they do not know why they act in certain ways."

The five whales searched for several days in all the bays and coves from Klemtu to the Pacific. It was exhausting work locating the rare and elusive Spirit Bear. Finally, Rainbow looked towards the shore and spotted the mysterious white bear with a golden stripe on its back. He was sleeping next to a stream.

"There, I see one," Rainbow said to the others.

All the whales were happy to finally see the last animal required as part of their quest. The Spirit Bear was always the most elusive animal for humpies to find. It was now time to swim to the ancient burial grounds.

They swam in a V shaped formation with Sitka in the lead. Like birds flying in the sky, the V shape made it easier for the whales following the first whale to swim. It took almost two full days for the five humpbacks to reach the spot where the ancient remains were located.

"We are here. It is a deep dive to reach the burial spot. We will enter the cave together. I promise there will be light and fresh air in the cave. Trust me. More importantly, trust in yourselves. Do not be afraid. You are mighty humpbacks. Stay close to me," Sitka told the others.

As the whales started their dive, Angel felt the presence of her mate in her mind and her heart. He was not physically close. His mind was focused on his family and others of his pod. Angel smiled to herself. Argonaut was keeping a watch from afar. Ever since she had been kidnapped the Inua had been more vigilant over their pod.

When the whales entered the cave and surfaced for air the four who were here for the first time were in awe of what they saw. The light was beautiful. The air was pure. In the waters below were more whale bones than could be counted.

Rainbow asked Sitka, "Why are the whale bones here and not somewhere else? What makes this place so special?"

Sitka replied, "I do not know why the first whales chose this place. Humans bury their dead in places where they lay close together. They chose green land their kind enjoy. The memory keepers talk of a secret burial place where large land animals, called elephants, go to die in a far-off place. I think it is part of our history. Like migrating to our winter home. There are things that are natural to us. We have always been this way and we do them, as is our habit. Not all whales have the choice to die here but many of us do. This place has a special sense of family and warmth. For me, it seems as if all the whales here are connected to us. Does that make sense to you?"

"It does. I feel the same sense of being among family here. There is safety and a feeling of eternity I cannot explain," Rainbow said.

The five whales spent time singing their favorite songs about love, respect, and family. Finally, Sitka signaled that it was time to leave. After one final look, the five whales left the cave of the ancients.

Angel said to Sitka, "Thank you for leading us on this quest. I feel closer to each of you and to all whales in our pod now than I did before we came."

"You are welcome dear friend. You may lead us home. I am tired and want to swim a little easier at the rear of the group," Sitka answered.

As the whales started the journey back to the sanctuary, they each knew they were going to be forever changed by the experience of their quest.

Angel reached out to Argonaut and said,

"Thank you mate, for keeping your Inua senses alert for us. I always feel safer knowing your spirit is close."

SPIRIT BEAR

ORCA GET MAD

It was late August. Tour boats were streaming to and from Alaska on the inside passage from Vancouver and Seattle. Spirit Bear Lodge was booked solid for the remainder of the season. Matt and Angie had all the guests they could accommodate aboard the Orcella 2 until the last tour in mid-September.

Reports were received from many locations around the world that orca were attacking boats. Kayaks, small boats, and even larger vessels were being rammed by orca. The large black fish were coordinating attacks on great white sharks in Australia and off-shore of Cape Town in South Africa. No one knew why the orca had suddenly decided to attack boats and great whites. If this behavior continued, humans were bound to react violently and hunt the orca.

Only one creature in the world could talk to both orca and humans. That one creature was the Inua Argonaut.

Wild Bill Mendenhall reached out to Argonaut and asked if he, Commander Pierstorff, Captain

DeFord, and Jason could meet the Inua the next morning at sunrise near Hanson Island. Argonaut agreed to be there at first light.

After everyone had arrived, Wild Bill asked Argonaut if he knew why orca were attacking boats.

"I have not asked any of the orca why they are acting strangely, but I will," Argonaut said.

The Inua cleared his mind. He reached out to a pod of transient orca that were swimming about ten miles south of Hanson Island.

"Friends, this is the Inua Argonaut. I have a question for you. Do you know why your kind is attacking boats and sharks?" Argonaut said.

"We have heard from our friends in every ocean of terrible things happening. Salmon are disappearing. More of us are being caught and dying in nets. Boats are everywhere and we can find no peace. We are chased, harassed, and even hunted in some places. The waters are getting too warm for us in many oceans. We have had enough. We are fighting back the only way we know how. We are striking the boats that disturb us and killing sharks out of anger," said the eldest orca.

Argonaut explained to his human friends what the orca had said.

Commander Pierstorff told Argonaut that there were about fifty-thousand orca in the world. About twenty-five hundred lived in the eastern part of the north Pacific Ocean.

"There is no way the orca can effectively fight humanity. If they continue their aggressive behavior then humans will react with violence," she explained to Argonaut.

"What would you have the orca do? They are fighting for their lives. It is a war between them and humans. My kind was saved by many humans working together. Can we help the orca as my kind was saved?" Argonaut said.

Wild Bill asked Argonaut to speak to the orca about an idea he had that might help the orca and prevent a violent confrontation with humans. The former Coast Guard officer explained his plan to Argonaut who relayed it to the orca.

"We do not speak to humans like you do. We are not Inua. We do not know the ways of land creatures. Words mean little to us. We need changes made now or we will continue our attacks. If we do not fight for changes, we will die," said the orca.

Mendenhall called Jill White Feather at Project HOPE headquarters on Klemtu. He told her his ideas for ways to help the orca.

Jill agreed to help. She first called Premier Guyaen. She explained the plan to help the orca. The Premier, who is a great friend to conservation causes, agreed to do everything he could to end the disturbances that were upsetting the orca. Her next call was to Secretary General Rothman at United Nations offices in New York. Secretary General Rothman also agreed to help with the orca dilemma.

Premier Guyaen and Secretary General Rothman scheduled an emergency meeting in Vancouver. Also invited to the meeting was the Secretary of the Interior of the United States and a representative of the Federal Office of Fisheries and Oceans of Canada. These four individuals would try and devise a plan to help alleviate the stresses on the worldwide orca population.

Jason Belliveau, Commander Mendenhall, Captain DeFord and Commander Pierstorff were also invited as ex-officio members of the initial working group. The meeting was set for August 10th at the Pan Pacific Hotel in Vancouver.

Argonaut understood Mendenhall's plan. He was not sure that such an undertaking could be implemented quickly enough or if it would be sufficient to please the orca. It was a start.

Something had to be done soon before humans drove the orca to extinction.

The combined membership of the United States, Canadian, and United Nations working group named their plan Operation Black Fish. The plan called for twenty-five 500 square mile boat and fishing free zones in oceans around the world to be identified as orca protection zones. No boats would be allowed to enter these zones for any reason except in matters of national defense. New quotas would be imposed on salmon and other fish harvesting in areas frequented by orca. There would be quiet zones established near orca breeding areas, where boat traffic noise would be restricted and boat speed limits reduced.

The United States Secretary of the Interior and the Canadian Chief Officer of the Federal Office of Fisheries and Oceans both pledged the full support of their departments. Premier Guyaen agreed to urge the Canadian government to cooperate in implementing and enforcing Operation Black Fish. Commanders Pierstorff and Mendenhall agreed to coordinate with the Canadian Coast Guard and the United States Navy to set up the orca safe zones near their countries.

Secretary General Rothman supported the proposal. He agreed to present the plan for approval by the General Assembly at the next regularly scheduled meeting to be held the following week.

Argonaut was listening to the meeting proceedings. He reached out to the human group and spoke, "This is the Inua. You have made a great start today. It is very important that the orca see significant changes immediately in human behavior. I know it won't be easy to change human actions, but the orca are magnificent creatures. They have feelings, memories, hopes, and love for their families. They are not so very different from humans. If there is anything, I can do to help with Operation Black Fish just reach out with your thoughts. I will be listening."

Premier Guyaen said, "No matter how many times the Inua speaks it is an incredible experience to listen to him."

Secretary General Rothman felt the same way. He told the group, "The Inua's message to the General Assembly has had a great impact on policies and decisions concerning climate change and pollution. We are making progress. With help from Project HOPE and the Inua I feel we have a chance to save the world. Operation Black Fish will provide tangible results for all to see. We can demonstrate human willingness to save our endangered world by helping the orca."

Argonaut cleared his mind and with the full force of his Inua power spoke to orca all over the world. He explained the plan that had been adopted by Canada and the United Sates. He told the orca that many very important humans were asking all countries to do more to make the lives of the orca easier and safer.

Many orca spoke to the Inua that day. Some were hopeful. Many were doubtful that any changes would occur. Some agreed to stop attacking humans. Others wanted to seek revenge on every creature and boat.

The Inua reminded the orca who wanted to fight humans that they would lose the war, even if they won small battles. Argonaut explained to the orca that humans had almost hunted humpbacks to extinction. He did not want the same fate to await the orca.

There was now, with the implementation of Operation Black Fish, at least some hope that changes would be made to improve the lives of the majestic killer whales.

ANGRY ORCA

A NEW GENERAL

O n Saturday morning, Matt and Angie finished cleaning the Orcella 2 after that week's tour had left. The decks were spotless. The glass windows were gleaming. The fuel tanks were full. The ship was ready for the next tour that would start on Monday.

Matt and Angie had booked tours for seventeen weeks in a row. Every trip was filled to capacity. Angie had quickly adapting to life on the boat. She was truly enjoying being part of Matt's crew. She was learning about the straits and all the wildlife of the area.

"How would you like to have dinner in Port Hardy tonight?" Matt asked.

Angie replied, "That sounds great. What time?"

"I will pick you up at 6 PM. I'll make reservations at Tucker's Fish House for 7 PM," Matt said.

At 6 PM Matt arrived in his truck. He picked Angie up at her rental condo for the drive north to Port Hardy.

Along the way they talked of the last few months and the guests they had met. Most of the guests had been on previous Orcella 2 trips. Repeat business is a great asset in the tour industry.

After they were seated at Tucker's Fish House, Matt handed Angie an envelope.

"What is this?" she asked.

Matt smiled and said, "I have a proposition for you. Read the contract and let me know what you think."

The wait staff took their drink and dinner orders. Angie started to read the proposal. She was stunned by what she read.

"Is this a joke?" she asked Matt.

"Nope. I am very serious. I want us to become partners. We can work five months a year in Telegraph Cove. After the tourist season ends in Canada, we take a month off. We then work five months doing tour excursions on our new boat harbored in Southern California then take another month off," Matt explained.

"How can we afford all this? You are still paying off the debt on the Orcella 2," Angie said.

"Not any more. My Mom and Dad gifted me the Orcella 2, the house, and the guest house. They wanted me to receive my inheritance while I was young enough to enjoy it. They get to stay in the house two months a year rent free while we are traveling. With no debt we can easily afford the new boat in California. Since you are a United States citizen there will be no restrictions on your working as the registered owner and licensed captain of our new boat," Matt explained.

Angie stared at Matt in shock.

"I am not qualified to be a ship's captain," she said.

As their dinner was being served, Matt explained that Angie had one year to earn her Captain's license before they started their cruises in the United States. She already knew more about navigation, first aid, and engines than anyone else he had worked with. She would need to study hard when they were not working. He volunteered to be her tutor.

It was a lot for Angie to absorb. She ate her dinner in silence and contemplated Matt's offer.

"I suppose you have a business plan?" she asked.

"Look on pages four and five of your packet. All the projections for revenue and expenses are in there. A budget is included covering everything I can think of," he said.

"I bet you even have a boat picked out, don't you?" she smiled at Matt.

"She is a fifty-two-foot Nordic Tug harbored in

Tacoma, Washington. She has just been through a complete update and refitting. She is a bargain at five-hundred-thousand dollars. The seller will hold the loan debt. He is offering us a low interest rate on a twenty-year loan with no prepayment penalty," Matt told Angie.

"Has the boat been appraised?" Angie asked.

"Of course, it has been appraised and inspected. She appraised at six-hundred-seventy-five-thousand dollars. The seller is an old friend of my father. The seller wants his boat to go to a good home," Matt said.

"Wow. This is a lot to take in. Do I have time to consider the idea?" she asked.

"There is no rush. The seller has agreed to hold the boat for us without a deposit for sixty days. By then, we will be finished with the Canadian season. Once we finish in Canada we can fly to Tacoma. We will inspect the boat. I even have a name picked out," Matt said with a smile.

"What name have you come up with?" Angie asked.

"The General," Matt replied.

They both laughed.

After finishing their meal, they started the return trip to Telegraph Cove from Port Hardy.

"Do you really think we can pull this off?" Angie

asked.

"We know a whale that has magical powers. You flew planes in combat and were a general. I have lived on the water my whole life. I know we can do this," Matt replied.

"Here, I have another folder for you to look at when you get home. It is a portfolio of pictures of The General. I bet you will love her as much as I do. Give the idea some thought and we will talk in a few weeks. You are the best crew member I have ever had. You are adapting and learning at an amazing pace," Matt told Angie.

"Thanks for the vote of confidence. This is a big commitment. I am ready for a new challenge. This may be exactly what I have been looking for. I promise to do my homework, review the numbers, and consider the options. Thank you for believing in me," Angie said.

Matt dropped Angie off at her condo in Telegraph Cove. He drove to his home on the cliff overlooking Johnstone Strait. For the first time in a long time, Matt felt something deep for a female friend. Maybe their business partnership would lead to more than friendship. Only time would tell.

RAINBOW SPEAKS TO ARGONAUT

Early one morning as the pod was feeding, Rainbow swam up to her grandfather, Argonaut. She asked if she could talk to him.

"Of course, Rainbow. You may talk to me at any time. You are my favorite granddaughter," the Inua said.

"I am your only granddaughter," Rainbow replied with laughter in her thoughts.

"That is true, but you are still my favorite. What would you like to talk about?" Argonaut asked.

"Are there any female Inua in the world? I want to be an Inua when I am as big as you," Rainbow said.

"I don't know the answer to your question. I have only met one other Inua and it was an old raven who was near death. He was the oldest Inua of all time," Argonaut said to Rainbow.

"I very much want to be famous. I want to help other creatures like you do," Rainbow said.

"I did not choose to be an Inua. It just happened. I see no reason why females cannot be Inua but it is not something you can make happen. Even if you are not an Inua, you still can do much to help others. Sitka is our matriarch and leads our entire pod. Her mother, Spirit, was our family's matriarch before her," Argonaut explained.

"You can speak to other creatures. You can see the future. You have powers that others do not. You may be the greatest whale of all time. Is there any hope that I can be famous and powerful like you?" Rainbow asked her grandfather.

"You grandmother was saved with the help of a female human that works with our friend Matt on the Orcella 2. She flew a machine in the sky to help us get Angel back. The same female helped us sink the ship trying to hurt us. The Kitasoo trying to save the world are led by a young female named Jill White Feather. A female doctor helped save the whale who needed a new pectoral fin. There is nothing that a male can do that a female cannot do," Argonaut told his granddaughter.

"Other creatures respect you as a great Inua. I will never have that same feeling of respect, if I am not an Inua," said Rainbow.

Argonaut was silent for a few moments. He knew this conversation was very important to

Rainbow. He wanted to help his young granddaughter be all she could be and not be disappointed if she did not become an Inua when she grew older.

"I met an eagle who was very sad because his mate had died. He was alone and did not want to live. His mate was not an Inua but to him she was the most important and powerful creature in his life. When your grandmother was kidnapped, I was scared and could not find her. I needed Jason, General Choate, the orca, great whites, and dolphins to help. Even as an Inua, I could not save Angel by myself. No creature is powerful enough to do all things. We all need help. Your father, T-Rex, your great grandfather, and Guardian have often helped me when there was danger. When your father was trapped in the net after saving your grandmother, we needed many humans to help us. Without Jason, Matt, and others your father would have died and you would never have been born," Argonaut explained.

"I think I understand. I can be a good whale, help others, be kind, brave, and strong even if I am not Inua," Rainbow said.

"Got it, kiddo. There are stories told by the memory keepers of many females exactly like that. There was a group of warriors called Amazons who were fierce fighters. There was a famous human female named Joan of Arc who led an army of soldiers. General Choate was a fighter pilot in several big battles in the sky. Many countries have been led by females. There is nothing you cannot do," Argonaut told his granddaughter.

"If I am not an Inua I cannot speak to other creatures," Rainbow said.

"You have learned to use the talking machine so you can speak to Matt and Jason. That is a start. Who knows, maybe someday there will be a machine that lets all creatures talk to each other," Argonaut said.

"Thank you, grandfather. I feel much better after talking to you. I may never be an Inua, but I am the favorite granddaughter of the most famous humpback that has ever lived. That is good enough for me," Rainbow said.

The two whales touched noses. Rainbow left to play with the other calves of the pod.

Argonaut did not tell his granddaughter of the great strain of seeing the future or the stress of listening to so many voices. Sometimes it seemed impossible to think with all the clamor in Argonaut's mind. It certainly wasn't easy being an Inua. Argonaut was not sure he would wish being an Inua on any other creature, especially his granddaughter whom he loved with all his heart.

Raven, Argonaut's son, swam up to his father. He asked if his father and Rainbow had a good visit.

"She is a bright, inquisitive, and determined young whale. She reminds me a lot of you when you were her age," Argonaut said to Raven.

Raven smiled and said, "She really wants to be an Inua like her grandfather, the famous Argonaut."

Argonaut said, "As we both know, I did not choose this path. It was chosen for me. Often, I wish I were not Inua. I do the best I can. The challenges are many."

Raven swam next to his father. He touched his pectoral fin to his father's side.

"The memory keepers will be telling stories of your adventures for many years to come," Raven said.

The pair made their way back to the pod. It was their turn for night-time patrol duty protecting the pod from dangers.

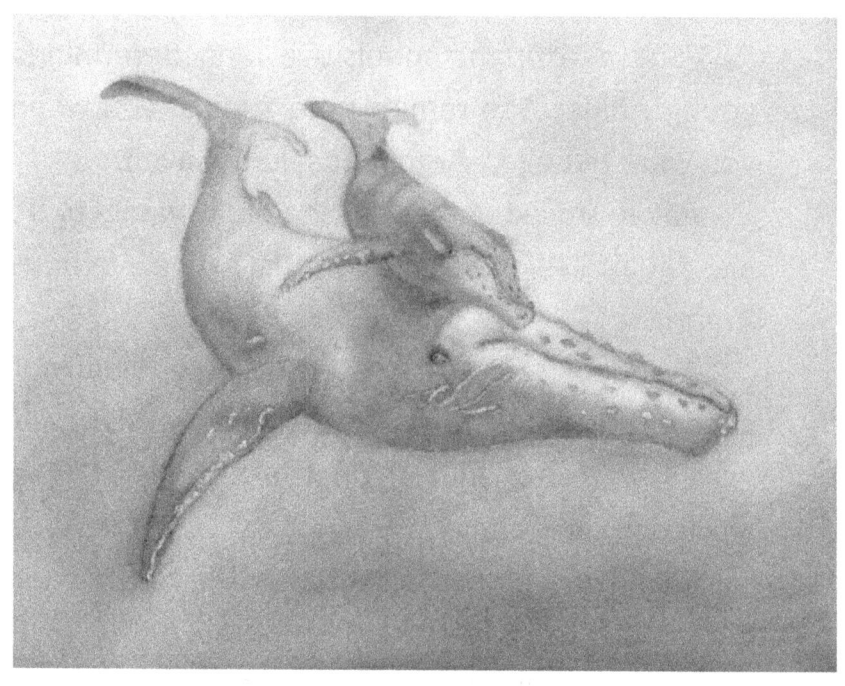

ARGONAUT AND RAINBOW

THE DREAM

The pod was resting after a busy day feeding. It was early August. The sun shone for long periods every day.

That evening, when most of the pod were sleeping, with half of their brains at a time as humpies do, all the whales had the same dream at the same time. Every whale, in his or her dream, saw two whales in danger. Both whales in the dream were badly hurt. Many humans were trying to save the injured whales. There was nothing the humpbacks could do to help. They all awakened. They nervously shared their dream with each other.

Raven asked his father if the story in the dream was the future that he had seen for himself.

"Yes, son. I am one of the two whales in the dream. I have already started to prepare for the future. All of our pod can now talk to Matt and Jason using the special machine. Your grandfather, T-Rex, and Guardian have promised to help Sitka if I die. You are strong, brave, and have proven to be a wonderful leader. Your mother may be matriarch someday. It may even be your mate, Biggsy, who leads our pod as matriarch in the future," Argonaut replied.

That same night, a different version of the dream occurred to many people in different locations. Humans dreamed of two whales being hurt. There was need for a major medical effort to save the whales. Procedures that had never been done before would be tried.

Dr. Skip Foster, Dr. Nancy Mendenhall, Dr. Ted Burns, Wild Bill Mendenhall, Captain Jim DeFord, and many others had the same humpback injury related dream. Matt Hawk and Jason Belliveau were on the Sadie Princess taking star trail pictures. They had the same dream while they were awake, as others had while sleeping.

Matt and Jason were several miles off shore taking pictures and videos of the stars. Jason looked at his friend and said, "I just had the strangest dream while I was wide awake."

Matt said, "I think I had the same dream. Two whales were seriously hurt. One or both of them might die."

Jason explained to Matt that several weeks ago, Argonaut had asked him to have another whale tail cover made. Argonaut wanted an A on the new cover, just like the A on his tail. Argonaut told Jason he was one of the whales who would be hurt. He may die.

"We cannot let Argonaut get hurt or possibly die. He has to flee into deeper water away from the sanctuary. He must stay safe," Matt said.

"He will not go. He says he will not run. If it is his destiny to die now, he wants to let it be in his sanctuary," Jason explained.

"We could kidnap him, tranquilize him, and drag him away from here. We have to do something," Matt exclaimed.

"Really? You expect to sneak up on an Inua and make him do something he does not want to do? Good luck with that theory. My guess is, he is reading our thoughts now. He would outsmart us at every turn," Jason told his friend.

They both heard the Inua speak, "You are right Jason. My home is here. I will live or die in these waters. I know both of you will help me, if you can. I, my entire pod, and many humans had the same dream. There is nothing we can do but wait."

Jason said, "The tail with the A is ready whenever you need it. How long before the accidents occur?"

Argonaut paused and said quietly to both his friends, "Soon, very soon."

Both Jason and Matt felt the trepidation in

Argonaut. They could only hope that the Inua would survive. They could not imagine a world without the magical Argonaut.

The future was becoming clearer to the Inua. He had an idea where the dream had come from.

Argonaut quieted his mind and reached far into the heavens and said, "Hello old friend, I thought you had died."

Hrafn laughed and replied, "I am no longer of your world. I am in the heavens as a star, but I still have some of my Inua powers. I wanted many to know of the danger you face. Everyone who will be involved needs to be prepared for all possibilities. It will take many people to help you and the other injured whale."

"Is this my time to die?" Argonaut asked the oldest Inua.

"Your death is one possibility. I know many people and many creatures will do their best to save you. I can see one whale dying and the other possibly surviving. It will be a dangerous time for you. All you can do is be brave and live each day to the best of your abilities. You are almost as powerful as I was, before I became a star. If any creature can survive this danger, I hope it is you," Hrafn spoke from the heavens.

"Thank you, great Raven Inua. I will do my best

to live up to your legend as a powerful and kind Inua. If I die soon, save me a space in the sky," Argonaut spoke to Hrafn.

More people started to receive and react to different versions of the dream. Commander Brient dreamt that he would need to coordinate two large vessels for operations on two injured whales. He would also need crane ships to lift the injured whales from the waters of the strait onto the ships.

Wild Bill Mendenhall dreamt of ferrying medical personnel in his helicopter to the site where the two injured whales lay.

Captain Jim DeFord saw himself transporting heavy equipment and supplies from Port Hardy to the medical incident location on his boat, Hercules.

Nurse anesthetists, surgeons, welders, medical technicians, pump operators, and many others dreamt of the events that would transpire somewhere in the Vancouver straits in the next few days.

No one knew when they would be needed. Everyone felt they would be needed soon. They each had an overwhelming urge to help save the injured whales.

LOGGING AND DANGERS TO WHALES

The laws protecting Canada's forests are among the strictest in the world. Loggers are granted a permit to harvest timber on public land. Forest management plans have to be approved before timber harvesting begins. The submitted plans must include provisions for reforestation of the harvested areas.

Vast quantities of timber are harvested in Canada each year. Logs are often shipped on huge barges in the waters along the western coast of Canada to the City of Vancouver.

Over the last decade many lumber mills have closed in British Columbia. The main causes of mill closures have been the devastation caused by the mountain pine beetle and the falling price of lumber. There is an agreement between Canada and the United Sates called the Softwood Lumber Agreement which limits price supports that can be offered by the Canadian government to loggers and mills. The agreement with the United States means the Canadian government cannot financially boost the price paid for timber, so mills have been forced to close. The lower sales price of timber limits or sometimes eliminates the profits made by the mills.

While many mills have closed, those still operating in western Canada often receive their raw material by long barges sent south from the logging areas. The barges are pulled by strong tug boats.

In early August 2022, the Westmaxx Barge Company of Vancouver was transporting eighty-thousand tons of logs on a barge called Trailing Mist. The barge was bult in 1964 in San Diego, California. The barge was pulled by an eighty-foot tugboat called Salty Dog.

The barge and tugboat were steaming to Vancouver from the forests of northern Canada when several chains holding the logs in place suddenly snapped. The barge was overloaded. Those loading the barge had not implemented all required safety rules and regulations. Efforts to save money, by lowering costs, had led the barge company to scrimp on safety measures. Over one-hundred giant logs fell from the Trailing Mist into the water with incredible force.

Just as the logs hit the water a humpback whale named Castor breached. The barge was being towed about two-hundred feet behind the tugboat. Castor thought he was safe to breach since he was not near the tugboat when he surfaced. The barge had no engine, so it was silent going through the water. An eighty-five-foot log weighing over twenty-five thousand pounds fell across Castor's spine with such force that it broke his back.

Castor was named after the Greek legendary figure who traveled aboard the famous boat, The Argo, with Jason and the Argonauts. Castor had trained Hercules in fencing. Castor was killed in battle. He was a favorite of the God Zeus. The ancient Greek gods allowed Castor of lore to live forever in either Olympus or in the Underworld.

As the humpback Castor lay in the water his fluke would not work. He had slight movement in his pectoral fins. The wake of the giant barge caused Castor to float to the beach of an island near Orca Lab. Castor felt no pain from his injury but he knew in his heart that he would never swim again.

Nakturalik, the eagle Argonaut helped after his mate died, saw the accident that crippled Castor. The eagle used his thoughts to reach out to the Inua.

"Argonaut, it is I, Nakturalik. Do you remember me?" he thought as he tried to contact the Inua with his mind.

"Yes, oh mighty eagle. We met several years ago after the loss of your mate," Argonaut replied.

"There has been a terrible accident. A humpback has been badly hurt by a falling log. The whale is stranded on the beach near where the humans listen for whales and orca. Do you know where that is?" Nakturalik asked.

"Yes, I do know the spot. Is the whale alive?" Argonaut asked.

"I can see his eyes move. There is some movement of his fins, but he is horribly injured. The whale needs help. Will you come?" the eagle pleaded.

"I am on my way. I will contact my human friends. I will ask my friends to meet us at the beach. Stay and watch the whale. Tell me if anything changes. Thank you, my eagle friend," Argonaut told Nakturalik.

Argonaut called Raven, T-Rex, and Guardian and told them that a whale was in need of help. The three friends started swimming with Argonaut south towards Orca Lab.

Argonaut reached out to Jason. The Inua explained that a humpback was seriously hurt and needed help.

Jason, Matt, and Angie boarded the Orcella 2.

They motored as quickly as possible south from Telegraph Cove towards Orca Lab.

Within thirty minutes the four whales and three humans met at Orca Lab.

Argonaut spoke to the injured whale. He asked what had happened. Castor explained about the falling log. Castor could not move his fluke. It was hard for him to breathe. Castor told the Inua he could feel nothing below his blowholes.

Argonaut explained to Matt, Angie, and Jason what had happened to Castor.

Jason got on his radio and called Commander Brient at the Port Hardy Coast Guard station.

Jason spoke to the officer, "Commander, we have a seriously injured humpback beached near Orca Lab. If Dr. Foster agrees to visit us and inspect the injury, will you arrange a helicopter flight to transport him?"

The commander said he could have a copter at the Pacifica Airlines terminal in thirty minutes.

"Let me know if Dr. Foster is available to fly to your location. I will wait to hear from you," the commander said to Jason.

Jason called Dr. Foster in Vancouver.

"Hi Jason. Let me guess. You have another emergency," said Dr. Foster.

"We have a badly injured humpback. I think his

spine may be broken. He can barely breathe. He cannot move his fluke. The whale has no feeling below his blowholes. I checked his heart rate and it is highly elevated. Commander Brient will have a helicopter transport you to our location, if you have time," Jason said.

"I will be at the Pacifica terminal in twenty minutes. I will bring enough drugs to put the whale to sleep and out of his misery," Dr. Foster told Jason.

"No. You will not kill this whale. I forbid it. He has a more important purpose to fulfill," said a booming voice in Skip Foster's head.

Jason heard what Argonaut had said to Dr. Foster.

"Do you know who that was," Jason asked.

Skip Foster said, "Either I am delirious or that was the famous Inua I have heard so much about. Why is he interested in an injured humpback?"

Jason was quiet for a moment. He told Dr. Foster he would let the Inua explain his interest in the injured whale, once the veterinarian was on site.

Jason called Commander Brient and arranged for the helicopter to deliver Dr. Foster to Orca Lab.

Castor reached out to Argonaut and said, "Am I going to die?"

Argonaut thought very carefully about his answer.

"Either you or I will die. Perhaps we both may join the ancients in death. I have seen this in a dream. It has been foretold by the ancient Inua Raven Hrafn. One of us may be able to save the other, with the help of humans. I do not fully understand what will happen, but I promise you will not suffer. Whichever one of us dies will be taken to the burial grounds of the ancients. My pod has instructions to take one or both of us to our final resting place. Trust me friend, I will do my best to save both of us. Part of my dream is that part of one of us lives on in the other. I do not understand this. I may be wrong. Help is on the way. Stay with me. I am by your side," said the Inua.

"I trust you great Inua. If it is my time to die, then I am ready. If your pod will take me to the ancient burial site then I will forever lie in peace," Castor said to Argonaut.

In about ninety minutes Dr. Foster arrived. He began to examine Castor.

After his examination he turned to Jason and said, "You were right. This whale's spine is severed. He will slowly die within a few days. It would be merciful to end his misery now."

"You heard the Inua. Something is going to

happen that involves both Castor and the Inua. We have to wait. Can you keep the whale comfortable and pain free?" Jason asked.

"I don't think he's in any pain since the spine is severed. His breathing will become more labored. He will starve or die of dehydration and that is a cruel way to treat an injured creature," Dr. Foster told Jason.

Jason said with great urgency, "We must keep this humpback alive. What can we do?" Jason asked Foster.

"We could feed and hydrate him intravenously. I will give him pain meds to keep him comfortable. How long must we keep him alive?" asked Dr. Foster.

Argonaut was nearby and heard what Dr. Foster said to Jason.

"Whatever is going to happen will happen within five sunrises. Can you keep the whale alive that long?" Argonaut asked Foster.

"I make no promises about the future of the injured whale. I will do my best to keep him alive and pain free for as long as I can, if it is that important. I will cancel appointments at my veterinarian practice for the next week. I will stay close to the injured whale. I will keep him comfortable and pain free," said Dr. Foster.

"Your best has always been good enough. I trust you," said Argonaut.

Dr. Foster was confused. How did the Inua know about him? Someone has a lot of explaining to do. He looked at Jason.

"Do you want to tell me how the Inua knows about me and what I do," Dr. Foster asked?

Jason asked Argonaut what he should do.

"Dr. Foster, look behind you," the Inua said.

Dr. Foster turned. Right behind him was Argonaut.

"I am Argonaut. I am the Inua. You have helped my kind many times. It is very important to keep my secret. I know we can trust you. Soon there will be another accident. I will be hurt. Castor and I will need you and many other humans to help us. Be ready doctor. The time is almost here," the Inua said to Dr. Foster.

Dr. Foster was stunned by his meeting with Argonaut. He felt compelled to do all he could to help this incredible being.

"Jason, it is time to put the tail cover with the A on this injured whale. You and Matt do it as quickly as you can. I will keep Dr. Foster's mind busy. He will not remember that the tail cover was put on Castor," Argonaut said.

Jason spoke, "I assume you are doing this so if

Castor dies the legend of Argonaut will die with him."

"You are right. If I die, then there will be no more Inua to protect. Hurry. The danger to me is very soon," Argonaut told Jason.

DEATH OF AN INUA???

There was no moon on the evening of Castor's accident. August is the peak viewing period for the Perseid meteor shower, as earth passes through the debris trail of the Swift-Tuttle comet. Perseid has more displays than any other comet.

The Perseids are the most popular meteor shower as they peak on warm August nights as seen from the northern hemisphere. The Perseids are active from July 17 to August 24. They reach a strong maximum on August 12 or 13, depending on the year. The Perseids are particles released from comet 109P/Swift-Tuttle during its numerous returns to the inner solar system. They are called Perseids since the radiant (the area of the sky where the meteors seem to originate) is located near the prominent constellation of Perseus, the hero, when at maximum activity. Perseus, in Greek mythology, slayed Medusa. Perseus also rescued Andromeda from a sea monster

Many boaters were in the Vancouver straits to

witness the meteor shower. Hundreds of what appeared to be shooting stars filled the night skies every hour.

Even the humpback whales were spyhopping to witness the lights flying across the sky.

The HighRider 150 is the first superyacht from the HighRider boat building company. It is capable of cruising without making any noise. The one-hundred-thirty-foot vessel can run exclusively from lithium polymer batteries. This means the ship makes no sound as it cruises if operating only on batteries.

On this night, the first HighRider 150 was doing sea trials in the deep strait channel near Orca Lab. The ship was named Hera. In Greek legend, Hera was queen of the Olympic gods. Many believed she was the wife of the most famous of all Greek gods, Zeus. The story of Greek gods is long and confusing.

Medea was something of a wizard who helped Jason of Greek legends get the golden fleece from her father, King Aeetes. Medea married Jason and used her powers to help him.

Jason broke his promise to love Medea forever. The legend says that Jason lost his favor with Hera. After falling from grace with Hera, Jason became lonely and unhappy. The famous Jason, who found the golden fleece, was asleep under the keel of the Argo when the rotting ship fell on him and killed him.

Argonaut the Inua humpback knew nothing of ancient Greek legends. He had a human friend named Jason and a son named Jason but that was just a coincidence. There happened to be a large ship sailing, without sound, near the location of Argonaut and Castor.

Suddenly Argonaut had a flash in his mind of the future. He turned and swam towards the west as fast as he could. His granddaughter, Rainbow, was feeding a short distance from the pod, just as the silent superyacht Hera was approaching. Rainbow started to spyhop. She was looking for a bait ball of fish when she felt a giant push in her back.

Argonaut saw in his mind the Hera silently approaching Rainbow. He could not let his granddaughter die. He swam from behind and pushed Rainbow away from the oncoming yacht. Just as Rainbow was out of harm's way, the Hera struck Argonaut on his right side. The Hera weighed over eight-hundred-thousand pounds. The yacht was more than ten times as heavy as Argonaut.

When the boat struck Argonaut, seven ribs on his right side were broken. Four of the ribs punctured his right lung causing severe damage. Argonaut was in grave danger of dying, as his right lung collapsed.

Hrafn saw the boat hit the giant humpback Inua. The ancient raven spoke to Jason and everyone else who had received the dream. The Inua raven told everyone what had happened. The raven explained that everyone needed to act now or the Inua of their world would die.

"Trust what you have seen in your dreams. You are needed to save a magnificent creature. If you succeed, you will be part of the most famous animal operation in history. Hurry before it is too late," Hrafn spoke. Everyone who would be involved in the tremendous undertaking to try and save one of the injured whales heard Hrafn and reacted immediately.

Dr. Foster agreed to stay with Castor. Matt and Jason steered the Orcella 2 across the strait to where Argonaut was floating near Orca Lab.

Argonaut was laying on his left side. He was unable to breathe because his right lung was badly damaged and his left blowhole was under water.

"Jason, please help me to lay flat in the water or I will die. I can hold my breath for a long time, but not forever," Argonaut said.

"I have no idea how to move an eighty-thousand-pound whale with no equipment. We need a lot of help right now," Jason said with fear in his thoughts.

Argonaut felt the presence of a large school of resident orca. He reached out to them and asked for their help.

"Great orca, I am gravely hurt. I need your help to lay straight in the water. My human friends are not strong enough. Will you help me?" Argonaut asked.

Six of the largest orca immediately swam to Argonaut. Three orca went on each side of Argonaut. They used their bodies to straighten the great humpback so both of his blowholes were out of the water.

"What shall we do with you now?" the eldest orca asked.

"Guide me across the harbor so I am beside the other injured whale. Many humans are coming to try and save both of us. I can move my fluke, but just a little. Only you, mighty orca can help me," Argonaut said.

The orca carefully guided Argonaut's helpless form across the bay. The six killer whales laid Argonaut in shallow water next to Castor.

"Is there anything else we can do for you, Inua?" the orca asked.

"No. Thank you for helping to save my life. I and my pod will remember this day. The memory keepers will tell stories of the orca that helped save the Inua. Be proud of yourselves. Share this story with all of your kind. Tell them how we, though different creatures, have helped to save each other," Argonaut said.

There were four-hundred-eighteen people who received the dream from Hrafn. They all had a role to play in trying to save Argonaut.

Ship captains, sailors, welders, engineers, machinists, crane operators, nurses, cardiac thoracic surgeons, anesthesiologists, and many more people started acting out their roles. This was to be the most complex and dramatic event of its kind in history.

Each individual knew exactly what they needed to do. Hrafn had left nothing to chance.

First on the scene were the CCGS Teleost and the CCGS Risley. These ships would serve as the main stages for the quickly unfolding events. Coast Guard helicopters began flying supplies and equipment to the two Coast Guard ships. Each ship had to be outfitted exactly like the other. The procedures on the two whales would be almost the mirror image of each other and occur simultaneously.

Two large crane barges left Vancouver. The crane barges were steaming as quickly as possible to the bay near Orca Lab where the two critically injured humpbacks lay side-by-side.

Three British Columbia ferries were loaded with ventilators, pumps, hundreds of feet of clear plastic hosing, generators, and over one-thousand containers of bottled oxygen.

A large fishing trawler, containing twenty tons of salmon, headed into the Johnstone Strait diverting from its planned route to Vancouver from Anchorage. The salmon was freshly caught. The fish from the trawler would be critical in the days ahead.

Flights of medical personnel from Vancouver made their way to the two Canadian Coast Guard ships. Supplies were unloaded from the ferries as they arrived by Canadian sailors and ferry personnel.

Commander Mendenhall helped transport personnel to the site using his helicopter. Captain DeFord brought supplies from the airport at Port Hardy to the two Coast Guard ships on his boat, Hercules.

Everyone knew exactly what they had to do even though these actions had never been performed on such large animals. Hrafn was guiding all the personnel with his ancient powers.

The two most important people who boarded the CCGS Teleost and CCGS Risley were Dr. Dan Knauf and Dr. Marie Gionet. These two surgeons were the most accomplished organ transplant specialists in Canada. They each had a surgical team with them.

Dr. Gionet, with her chief fellow, Dr. Anne Marie Peacock would be the procurement specialists. They would attempt to procure the right lung from Castor. Dr. Dan Knauf and his team would attempt to remove Argonaut's damaged lung and replace it with the lung procured from Castor.

More and more equipment and supplies arrived. Technicians, surgical assistants, anesthesiologists, and pulmonary specialists from Seattle and Vancouver boarded the ship. Two mobile Magnetic Resonance Imaging (MRI) machines arrived by ferry. One was unloaded onto each of the two coast guard ships. One MRI would be necessary to help the surgeons understand the internal damage Argonaut had suffered. The second MRI would help guide the surgeons in removing Castor's lung.

The preparations were occurring at a frenetic pace. Cables, lights, and all types of equipment covered every inch of the decks of both ships. Fortunately, the weather was calm and the strait was tranquil.

Both whales were conscious. Castor asked Argonaut what was happening.

"Your back is broken. It cannot be healed. You cannot swim. You will never be able to move," Argonaut told Castor.

"This means that I will die here," Castor said.

"I don't have the power to save you. My human friends are the bravest and smartest of their kind. There is nothing they can do to help you," Argonaut said with a heavy heart.

Castor looked at Argonaut lying next to him and asked, "Are you badly hurt?"

The Inua told Castor, "I was hit by a boat while saving my granddaughter. I may die here beside you, if the humans cannot find a way to fix me. They have a plan but I don't think I can allow them to try their idea."

"Why don't you want your friends to try and save you?" Castor asked.

Argonaut felt great sadness in his heart. He owed Castor the truth. He would not lie.

"To save me, the humans need to take part of your body and put in me. If this works, I may live. I could also die, as this procedure has never been done on a humpback before," Argonaut explained.

"If I am certain to die would it not be better for me to try and save the life of an Inua, by giving you part of me? What use will my body be when I am dead? It would be a waste of my life if I do not help save yours. I am willing to give part of me to save you. It would be an honor to give of myself to help you, who has done so much to help so many others," Castor said.

"We may both die, my friend. I cannot see into the future about what will happen with us," Argonaut said.

"Can you tell me what will become of me?" Castor asked.

Argonaut asked Dr. Knauf to explain the operations to him so he could tell Castor exactly what was going to occur.

Dr. Knauf explained, "First, we will place tubes down each of your blowholes to help you both breathe. Since you cannot breathe if you are asleep, these machines will breathe for you. Once the machines are working, we will give you a strong sedative which will put you to sleep. We will insert long needles attached to tubes into your bodies to keep oxygenated blood circulating to all your organs. We have machines to oxygenate your massive bodies and a large emergency supply of bottled oxygen. Once you are asleep, we will use giant plasma cutters to cut an opening on the right side of each of you. One team of doctors will start to remove Castor's lung and the other team will remove Argonaut's broken ribs and then remove his right lung.

"As soon as the second team has removed Argonaut's lung then the lung from Castor will be inserted into Argonaut's body. We will then tie off hundreds of blood vessels. We suture the new lung into place. We hope we do not injure any other vital organs during the operation.

"Argonaut will lose a lot of blood during the operation. He may need a transfusion of blood and the only available source will be Castor. Once Castor's lung is removed, we may need to start pumping blood from Castor to Argonaut.

"We know virtually nothing about blood groupings in humpbacks. Any transfusion might be enough to kill the recipient whale.

"At some point, when any required blood has been transferred to Argonaut, we will increase the anesthesia flowing into Castor. The increased anesthesia will allow Castor to die peacefully.

"If we can get the new lung inserted into Argonaut, if the blood transfusion is successful, if we do not damage any other organs, then a team of veterinarian orthopedic specialists will insert replacement ribs into Argonaut. The new artificial ribs are made of tungsten to replace the ones broken when Argonaut was hit by the ship.

"If Argonaut survives the operation, we will slowly reduce the pumping of oxygen into him. Hopefully, after the operation, he will be able to breathe on his own.

"The truth is there is very little chance that this plan will work. The operation is likely to take several days given the massive size of the lungs. The complexities of learning how to do this for the first time is overwhelming. We have done this many times on humans but everything is different in humpbacks."

Argonaut explained everything that Dr. Knauf had said to Castor.

"When I die, will there be any pain?" Castor asked.

The Inua repeated the question to Dr. Knauf.

"Castor will be totally asleep while under anesthesia. When we have removed his right lung, we will increase the anesthesia until his heart stops. He will never feel any pain. I promise," explained the surgeon.

Argonaut felt as if his heart would break. How could he ask another whale to die so that he might have a chance to live? There must be another way.

Hrafn read Argonaut's thoughts and said, "Castor will die regardless of the choice you make. The only wise decision is to try the operation the humans have suggested if you want a chance to live. Inua, your work in the world is not done. Your family and your pod need you. I see you doing great things for many creatures, if you survive. I hope you do not let Castor's life be wasted. He can give you the gift of life. What greater gift can one creature give to another?"

Castor heard Hrafn's thoughts and said, "Inua raven, I am ready to try and help save Argonaut. I have led a good life. It is my time to go to the cave of the ancients. I want to help the Inua."

Argonaut reached out with his left pectoral fin and touched Castor.

"If I live, we will forever be part of one another. Every breathe I take will be partly you living in me. Every beat of my heart will be because of you. My pod, my mate, my son, and my granddaughter will owe you everything. I promise that whatever happens, my pod will take you to the ancient humpback whale burial grounds to be with our ancestors. Your memory will live forever among the stories of the memory keepers. You will be famous, as the hero who saved the Inua," Argonaut said.

"I am ready, great Inua. Tell your friends to begin. I hope you live to do more good things for our world," Castor said.

ARGONAUT STRUCK BY THE YACHT HERA

THE OPERATIONS BEGIN

The CCGS Teleost and the CCGS Risley were tied together not far from Telegraph Cove. The Canadian government had banned all travel on the watery passage near the ships until the operations on the two whales were completed. British Columbia ferries and tour boats had to make a one-mile detour to the east to avoid the site of the unfolding dramatic events.

The team set to procure the undamaged lung from Castor was headed by world famous cardiac thoracic surgeon Dr. Marie Gionet. She had trained at Harvard Medical School and completed her fellowship training under Dr. Knauf at the University of Florida.

Dr. Knauf would be leading the team removing the damaged lung from Argonaut's right side. Dr. Knauf would be performing the transplant into Argonaut once Castor's lung was available.

Dr. Maura McDonnell, the chief orthopedic surgeon, would be removing Argonaut's damaged ribs and inserting the tungsten replacements once the new lung was in place. Stryker corporation of the United States offered free titanium plates and screws to attach the new ribs to Argonaut's spine. Stryker is renowned for hip, shoulder, and knee replacement parts in humans. No implants of this size had ever been manufactured before.

Castor was placed under general anesthesia. Before he was fully asleep two hoses were gently placed down his blowholes into his left lung. Separate pumps were attached to each hose. One hose would pump five-hundred gallons of air every ten minutes into Castor. The other pump would pump used oxygen from Castor at the same rate. These pumps were coordinated by a computer that had each machine working separately but in timed coordination with the other.

Two giant intravenous lines were inserted into Castor using different main arteries. One line was used to withdraw blood from the whale. The blood was circulated through an oxygenator. The machine cleaned the carbon dioxide from Castor's blood. The second line from the machine returned highly oxygen rich blood back into the whale.

Emergency tanks of oxygen were on site in case of failure of the oxygenator.

The combined processes of pumping oxygen into Castor and also giving him high oxygen concentrated blood were designed to keep his heart pumping and his vital organs functioning.

Just as Castor was falling asleep from the anesthesia, he heard Argonaut say, "Thank you for the gift of life. Whatever happens, there will be a new star named Castor in the heavens tonight."

Dr. Gionet used the plasma cutter to make a large incision into Castor's right side. She had previously reviewed the MRI scans of his body. She and her team knew exactly where his right lung lay. The cutter was so hot that it sealed the veins as it was making the incision. There was minimal blood loss as a result of the incision. Robotic scalpels were inserted into the incision. Each robot moved to a different spot and began separating Castor's lung from his body. The scalpels were controlled by computers that were operating under Dr. Gionet's supervision. Each robot was equipped with an infrared night vision camera so even inside the dark cavity of Castor's body, Dr. Gionet could see what was happening.

Once Castor's lung was detached, the robots each took a portion of a large fine mesh net made of braeon and tungsten and inserted it into Castor's body. This netting was made to hold the lung as it was removed by a crane from Castor. The material had proven effective in giving support to the prosthesis fitted to Valent's left pectoral stub. The robots wrapped the netting around Castor's lung.

Dr. Knauf used exactly the same procedure to make the incision into Argonaut. An oxygenator was in use. Pumps for giving Argonaut oxygen and removing carbon dioxide through his blowholes were in place. The Inua was fast asleep. Argonaut's breathing was done for him by machines.

Three robots preformed the same procedure of cutting away Argonaut's damaged lung from his body. Dr. Nancy Mendenhall and Dr. McDonnell had previously removed Argonaut's broken ribs.

Once the robots finished the surgery, they pulled an identical net around Argonaut's damaged lung. Dr. Knauf supervised the lifting of the collapsed lung from Argonaut. The lung was placed in the hold of a large crab fishing ship that was standing by. Argonaut's lung would be transported, in the extremely cold hold of the ship, to the University of Canada in Vancouver to be studied by veterinarians. An entire lung from a living humpback had never been available for research before.

Humpback whales do not get cancer. The veterinarians and cancer specialists at the University of Canada in Vancouver were hoping to unlock the mystery of why whales do not get the disease. They would perform in-depth analysis of Argonaut's lung. The chief researcher was Dr. Bruce Stechmiller, an oncologist who trained at John Hopkins University. Pieces of Argonaut's lung were to be shipped to sixteen oncology centers in North America for research into the cancer resistance of humpback whales.

Researchers have been studying whale genetics to unlock the cancer resistance in humpbacks for many years. Elephants are also resistant to cancer. Dinosaurs did get cancer. Studying Argonaut's lung may help cancer researchers find a cure for cancer in humans. Having such a large amount of Argonaut's lung tissue to study may help scientists understand the reason some species are cancer resistant.

Once the lung had been removed from Argonaut and deposited into the freezing hold of the crab ship, Dr. Gionet directed the crane to remove the lung from Castor. The crane carefully lifted the lung from Castor and placed it next to Argonaut.

Dr. Knauf directed the operators of the second crane to position the lung donated from Castor into the open cavity on Argonaut's right side. The team of surgeons and nurses began the long process of sewing the new lung into Argonaut. The lung had to be attached to the nasal duct and multiple arteries and veins.

Whales cannot breathe through their mouth because, unlike land mammals, their digestive system and respiratory system are not connected. The blowhole leads to the nasal duct. When the muscles involved in breathing are relaxed, the blowhole is closed by fibrous plugs, like flaps, that prevent water from entering the respiratory system. The whale must actively open its blowhole by tightening the muscles of the blowhole. Unlike land mammals, breathing in whales is not automatic. Whales have to think about each breath they take.

The threads used to stitch Argonaut's new lung in place were woven from braeon. Cameras attached to robotic arms were used by the surgical team to see where to sew. Long robotic arms with needles threaded with the miracle braeon thread were operated by remote control to do the stitching. This exacting process had never been attempted before on an animal as large as

Argonaut. A stich a millimeter was required. Over thirteen-thousand stiches would be made to securely attach the new lung.

Dr. Gionet alternated stitching with Dr. Knauf and Dr. Peacock. The operation continued for eighteen hours. Once the surgeons were happy with their work, the clamps that blocked the flow of blood and oxygen to Argonaut's right lung were removed.

Dr. Marisa Mendenhall, her mother Dr. Nancy Mendenhall, and Dr. Maura McDonnell inserted and attached Argonaut's new ribs. Over time, if all went according to plan, new bone would grow over the plates and screws. The doctors hoped Argonaut's rib cage would be as strong as it was before the accident.

Both whales were placed on large tarpaulins before their operations. The tarp under Castor would be wrapped around his body and sewn together so he could be taken by the Sitka pod to his final resting place in the burial cavern of the ancients. Argonaut's tarp would be used to help keep his incision from opening.

Dr. Knauf and Dr. Gionet had the crane lift the tarp into place around Argonaut and help bring the pieces of surgically cut skin closer together leaving just enough room for them to use more braeon thread to suture the incision made into Argonaut's side. Another eight-thousand stitches were required to seal the incision made by the plasma cutter.

Dr. Ted Burns, the famous plastic surgeon, performed the last step I sealing the incision in Argonaut's right side with stitches designed to dissolve over time. The doctors hoped to have as little scaring as possible remain after the incision healed.

Once the wound had been stitched, a polymer film was placed over the area. Polyurethane was applied over the polymer film to act as a fast-drying cement. Once the cement had dried, the vest like tarp was fitted tightly around Argonaut. Within two hours of the last stich being made, the team was ready to see if the operation on Argonaut was successful.

The needles attached to the oxygenator lines were removed. The two hoses used to keep Argonaut breathing were withdrawn. All anesthesia was stopped. An injection of adrenalin was given to Argonaut to stimulate his return to consciousness.

Everyone on both teams watched and waited. For several minutes there was no movement of Argonaut's body. Finally, he exhaled a giant breathe from his blowholes and inhaled deeply. His eyes opened. His heart was beating normally.

Argonaut could read Dr. Knauf's mind. He knew he was in for a long and slow recovery, but he was alive and had a new lung. His chances of survival were good.

Dr. Skip Foster was standing by Castor. At his signal, the machines pumping air into Castor's left lung were stopped. The anesthesiologist who had controlled the oxygen flowing into Castor increased the level of phenobarbital passing into the blood stream until Castor quietly died in peace and without pain.

Just as Castor's heart beat for the last time, a giant rainbow appeared over the two ships. Argonaut reached out to Hrafn and thanked him for the tribute to Castor's sacrifice.

Hrafn said to Argonaut, "Castor's spirit is in the sky. There is a new star in his honor that will shine forever. He will always be remembered by the memory keepers as the whale who saved the Inua Argonaut. There is no greater gift one creature can give to another than part of himself. Use the gift wisely Argonaut."

OPERATIONS BEGIN ON CASTOR AND ARGONAUT

CASTOR'S FUNERAL PROCESSION

Now that Argonaut was awake from his surgery, he could explain to Angel, his sons Raven and Jason, his granddaughter Rainbow, and the entire pod what happened to him. He told them how Castor had given him a lung. Now, thanks to the gift of life from Castor, Argonaut was able to breathe normally.

Sitka asked when Argonaut would be back in the water with his family.

"I don't know. The humans say it will be many sunsets and sunrises before they know for sure if I am going to live," Argonaut replied.

Angel asked her mate if he was in a lot of pain.

"The pain I feel is only temporary. I know that you are near. Knowing that my family and my pod are close makes everything better," Argonaut told his mate.

Raven asked his father how he was going to eat while lying on the big ship.

Argonaut explained the humans were going to grind up fresh salmon from a nearby boat and feed him through a big tube every day until he was able to swim again and feed himself.

"I have a very important job for you, the Inua said to Knolhval. I would like you, T-Rex, Biggsy, Raven, Jason, Orion, Star, and Hval to take Castor's body to the ancient burial cave. I am alive with part of him in me. I will ask the orca, dolphins, and great whites to join you. I want Castor's last swim to be one that will be told by memory keepers for all time," Argonaut explained.

Knolhval told his son, "It will be done as you have asked, you have my promise. We will take turns pulling the body of Castor to its final resting place. Call to the great whites as we leave the harbor. Ask the orca and dolphins to meet us where the strait enters the ocean."

Argonaut asked his friend Jason to have the humans lift Castor's body into the water. Four long lines were tied around Castor's pectoral fins so that four whales could, in unison, tow the body out to sea.

A solemn procession began as the whales started the long slow journey to the sacred burial cave. Once the whales reached the harbor entrance, the orca, dolphins, and great whites joined in the burial cortege.

The humpbacks took turns pulling the rope. The whales who were not pulling sang ancient whale songs of sadness for the loss of a friend. The song carried for many miles. The great whites, orca, and dolphins followed the whales in a V shaped formation.

Finally, the whales arrived at the burial site.

Argonaut was following events from the ship. He thanked his friends the dolphins, great whites, and orca. All the other mammals and sharks circled the whales as a form of honor guard as Castor was taken to the burial cave.

All the humpbacks dove down to the cave. The humpbacks removed the ropes from Castor's body. Each whale was alone with his or her own thoughts.

Biggsy knew she was alive because Argonaut asked his human friends to save her. Knolhval had rejoined his family after Argonaut reached out to him. Orion, Star, and Hval were part of the pod because Argonaut had accepted them and taught them about the kind and honorable life a whale could lead. Raven was glad that his father had reached out to his human friends to save him from the net. T-Rex was Argonaut's oldest friend. Argonaut had asked T-Rex to join the Sitka pod. Joining the pod forever changed the life of the massive T-Rex. Jason, Argonaut's second son, heard the stories of his father's many exploits. Rainbow, Argonaut's granddaughter, learned from her grandfather that she could be a great whale even if she never became an Inua.

All the whales knew the Inua was alive because of the sacrifice Castor had made. The whales sang one last song of goodbye. The humpbacks slowly returned to the surface.

All the animals involved in the funeral swim started the long journey back to the Vancouver straits. The dolphins swam ahead as did the orca. The great whites split away before the entrance to the harbor. The humpbacks returned to the strait to be near Argonaut.

Knolhval told Argonaut, "We have done as you have requested. Castor is among the ancients and will, for eternity, live in peace."

Argonaut told his friends and family to go feed and rest. It had been a long few days. The entire pod needed to eat and sleep.

"I will be fine. The humans will take good care of me. The ancient Inua Hrafn is still watching over me. Don't worry," Argonaut told the pod.

THE TRANSPLANT STORY IS TOLD

Argonaut knew the transplant story could not be kept secret. Too many people had been involved. There was no way he could erase so many memories involving such a long period of time.

Argonaut reached out to his friend, Brigitte Fisher, who knew his Inua secret. Ms. Fisher had kept the Inua secret when she was a reporter. The whale knew he could trust her to tell the truth about the operations. Argonaut wanted the story of Castor's sacrifice told so the entire world would understand what the gift of life from organ donation means to the recipient and his or her family.

"Do you remember me?" Argonaut reached out with his thoughts to Fisher.

"Of course, I remember you. I have been reading about a whale organ transplant procedure happening near Telegraph Cove. Did that have anything to do with you?" she asked.

Argonaut explained the facts of the story. He told Fisher how Castor was hurt by a falling log that broke his spine. Argonaut had been hit by the silent boat. One of Argonaut's lungs was severely damaged. Humans had taken a lung from the dying Castor and put it inside Argonaut.

"I want you to write a story. Explain how humans saved one whale, me, by using the lung of a whale who would not live. Jason had a tail cover made for Castor with an A on it. The world should think that the humpback Argonaut has died. Many humans have pictures of Castor's printed tail showing the A. I still have the tail cover hiding the A on my fluke. If you tell the story about the death of Argonaut, my secret will be safe from those who have heard of my adventures. Will you do this for me?" the Inua asked.

"This is the story of a lifetime. It will be the greatest piece I have written. I am registered as an organ and tissue donor. I believe in the cause. When people read of one whale saving another it will have a huge impact. Will you tell me the whole story from the beginning?" Fisher asked.

Argonaut explained how he wore a tail cover so he would not be recognized. He was now known as Michael. He told Fisher about how he felt the impending danger. Jason had the new tail cover printed with the A. The new tail cover was put on Castor soon after he was struck by the log.

Argonaut told Fisher of his conversations with Castor before the operations. Argonaut explained that Hrafn used his ancient powers to inform humans, in their dreams, of their involvement in the transplant.

Fisher agreed to contact Dr. Knauf for an interview about the transplant.

"I promise you, Dr. Knauf will be happy to give you the interview. I have some influence over people. I am certain he will speak with you," Argonaut said.

Within a few days, Ms. Fisher met with Dr. Knauf at the Vancouver Fairmont hotel. She interviewed him for more than three hours about the twin operations.

"The scope of what the surgical teams did is unprecedented. Cooperation between such large groups, requiring precise timing, was a challenge. We did things not dreamed of until now. Robotic scalpels, miniature drones, huge cranes, braeon for sutures, and many other complexities made this a momentous event," Dr. Knauf explained.

"What are the benefits for humans?" Fisher asked.

Dr. Knauf thought for a few moments and said, "Now we know we can operate on a grand scale. We have utilized new procedures and materials which may be scaled down to size, for use in humans. As more species reach the brink of extinction, we may be called upon to save other large and small animals with operations like these."

"Who paid for the costs of these procedures?" Fisher asked.

"The National Geographic Foundation, Sea Shepherd Conservation Society, Greenpeace, Sierra Club, Whalewatch, and the World-Wide Fund for Nature all contributed. The United Nations, Canadian Government, and several private donors helped. All the labor was provided, at no cost, by the medical staff, technicians, and countless volunteers," Knauf replied.

"Was it worth the time and money?" Fisher asked the surgeon.

"I have been involved in many heart and lung transplants in humans. My teams and I often grasp life from the clutches of certain death. Donors and their families have given so much that others may live. This transplant involving two humpback whales may lead to greater awareness of the need for more human donor registrations. The increased sensitivity of the need for more donors alone is worth the time and cost involved in this transplant. Death is not a subject we like to discuss. However, planning for the eventuality is something we all should do in advance," Dr. Knauf explained.

Fisher thanked the surgeon and started to write the story. Within twenty-four hours her article on the whale lung transplant was making headlines in every newspaper around the world. Donor registrations across the globe were rapidly increasing, as more people read the story of one whale giving life to another.

Argonaut knew how the story was impacting the human world. He was proud that his suffering, and even the death of Castor, had led to good things happening to humans. The more humans registered as organ donors the fewer people would die while waiting for a transplant.

Fisher did a series of follow-up stories. She reported how local fisherman were providing salmon for Argonaut (she had to call him Michael) to eat, while recuperating on the CCGS Teleost. The Inua remained on the ship as his wound healed. She explained once the doctors were ready, Argonaut (alias Michael) would be lowered into the waters near Klemtu. The Kitasoo had agreed to watch over the whale. They would help feed him, until he was strong enough to feed on his own. Dr. Foster stayed on the CCGS Teleost for two weeks. He monitored Argonaut's vital signs to make sure there were no indications of infection or organ rejection.

Drs. Gionet, Knauf, Peacock, Foster, Burns and Mendenhall all were satisfied with the results of the transplant operation.

Humans who receive an organ transplant often are required to take many anti-rejection drugs for the rest of their lives. Since this was the first whale-to-whale organ transplant, it was unknown if Argonaut's body would accept or reject the transplanted lung. The blood transfusion from Castor to Argonaut was the first of its kind. Unlike human transfusions, there apparently is no blood-type matching issues in whale transfusions or the surgeons may just have been lucky this time. For now, it appears the donor and recipient whale had matching blood characteristics.

For her reporting Ms. Fisher was awarded the Canadian Hillman Prize. The Hillman is an award honoring investigative reporting that causes change on the issue being reported. Clearly, with the record number of new organ donor registrations, Fisher's reporting was having a dramatic effect; not only in Canada but throughout the world.

The scientist Bruce Rogers, read about the death of Argonaut (really Castor). He abandoned the idea that Argonaut was a magical whale.

Argonaut was happy that his secret would remain safe, at least for a while longer.

NEW HOPE - MORE CHALLENGES

The six young directors of Project HOPE, along with Commander Mendenhall and Captain DeFord, were in their regular weekly board meeting. Charles Windsong presented an update on an idea he had been working on.

"I have narrowed down the list of potential interns, for us to mentor, to the ten names on the list each of you has in your agenda. I have ranked them based on the criteria we discussed. All potential interns have outstanding academic and volunteer credentials. If the group agrees I would like to call a vote on the issue. I propose we invite the top six rated individuals to join us in Klemtu for four weeks. During this time, they can shadow us. We can mentor these young volunteers to possibly follow in our footsteps, as we begin a transition to new leadership over the next two years," Windsong said.

Mary Raven seconded the proposal. The motion was unanimously approved. Commander Mendenhall agreed to contact the potential interns and arrange for their travel to Klemtu. One applicant was from eastern Canada. One applicant was from southern France. An Indian student from New Delhi was on the list. Another intern was from Brazil. One intern would betraveling from Beijing, China. The final name on the list was Johnny Eagle from Haida Gwaii. The group was pleased that a neighbor would be part of the intern mentorship program.

The Project HOPE directors knew they needed to broaden the base of leadership to include more countries and people of more diverse backgrounds. Hopefully, the interns would apply for leadership positions in Project HOPE, when elections were held.

Jill White Feather presented a report on recent climate change news. The United States was suffering from dramatic ever-increasing damage to the coral reefs surrounding the country. The damage to the reefs may well be irreversible. The good news is the new administration elected in 2020 decided the United States would rejoin the Paris Climate Accord. This was encouraging as many other countries would likely follow the lead of one of the world's largest economies, in supporting better climate control rules and regulations.

Another part of Jill's report focused on the harm caused to many different mammals who live in the water from the COVID-19 pandemic. Human waste had entered the waters of the world. Studies have shown that at least fifteen marine mammal species are susceptible to SARS-Covid type diseases. Many of these animals are already threatened. New pandemics might accelerate the risk of extinction for certain animals.

"The COVID-19 pandemic is a warning. If the world does not take the risk of diseases like COVID-19 more seriously and devise treatments sooner then more animals face extinctions. We need to lobby for more cooperation, communication, and vaccine availability to all countries," Jill stated.

The board approved a motion to formally lobby the United Nations for the formation of a new committee to address the effects of pandemic type illnesses on marine life.

ARGONAUT'S LONG ROAD TO RECOVERY

Two weeks after the lung transplant the crane barge tied to the CCGS Teleost lifted the Inua from the deck. The huge crane deposited Argonaut into the harbor next to Great Spirit Bear Lodge. The harbor was deep and narrow. There was little boat traffic in the area now that the lodge had closed for the season. The Inua would be safe in these protected waters. The Kitasoo would help feed the Inua while he regained his strength. Commander Brient promised increased Canadian Coast Guard air and patrol boat activity in the area to keep people and boats away.

Sitka and others of her pod stayed close to Argonaut. The pod helped lift the Inua's spirits. He was not used to being so inactive. The Kitasoo tribe netted krill to feed Argonaut. Dr. Foster flew from Vancouver every few days, aboard Commander Mendenhall's helicopter, to check on Argonaut's progress.

The incision seemed to be healing and the braeon stitching was holding. The mesh covering Argonaut's midsection was still in place. All vital signs were normal. There did not appear to be any signs of organ rejection. Things could not be going any better.

In late September, Argonaut asked Jason how much longer he would need to remain still in the waters near Klemtu.

"Dr. Foster said at least two more months for the ribs to be protected by new bone growth. The wound has to heal completely before you can swim and feed," Jason told his Inua friend.

"I can't wait two months. The pod has to leave for our winter home. The water will be too cold for any calves that are born here. I cannot risk the lives of our young by asking the pod to stay with me. I have to be ready to leave soon. I must go when the pod leaves," Argonaut said.

"I have an idea," said Jason.

"Half the pod including any pregnant females leave for migration when it is time. You and the other half of the pod spend the winter here. You can stand the cold. Your father lived for years in much colder waters. I can ask United States Admiral Rene Lee Pack and Captain Steve Waters to have a US Navy vessel accompany the pod to

Hawaii to help protect them. You can watch over the pod using your Inua powers from here. You could alert the pod to any danger. Does this plan seem ok to you?" Jason asked.

The Inua was reluctant to split the pod into groups. Argonaut knew, however, he was not strong enough to swim over three-thousand miles to the pod's winter home.

"The decision must be Sitka's. She's the matriarch of our pod. If she agrees, then I will stay here until the pod returns when the weather is warmer. Talk to your human friends. See if they are willing to send a ship to help protect the pod, in my absence. Thank you, old friend," Argonaut said.

Sitka agreed with the plan. The pod was preparing to leave for Hawaii On October 1st. Argonaut's family approached him one at a time. Each whale in turn rubbed noses with Argonaut.

"Do you think you can stay out of trouble while we are gone?" Angel asked her mate.

"Why are you going with the pod? Why don't you want to stay with me in our sanctuary?" Argonaut asked.

Angel smiled and said, "We are having another calf this season. I must go to the warm waters. It will be easier for me if I know you will behave yourself and not do anything foolish."

Argonaut beamed with pride at the news of another calf being born into his family.

"I promise to be quiet. I will let others care for me until you return. I have a name I would like to call our new calf, if you agree" Argonaut said.

"And what name would you give to our new calf?" Angel asked.

"If the calf is a male, we should name him Castor. If it is a female, we should call her Leah Castor, if you approve," Argonaut replied.

Angel was very pleased with Argonaut's suggestion of names for the new calf.

"You are so wise and kind. You are a wonderful mother. I will be watching and listening. I will know when our new calf is born. My body will be here, but my spirit will always be with you until the end of time," Argonaut told Angel.

Raven swam to his father and said, "My brother, grandfather, and I promise to care for the pod as you would. We will use all the wisdom you have taught us to keep the pod safe."

"You are wise for one so young. I trust you to be one of the leaders. Help Sitka with anything she asks. T-Rex, Guardian, and the others will be there with you. Remember all you have learned. Come back to me after the calves are born," Argonaut told his son.

At first light the pod started from the waters near Klemtu. Orion, Star, Rainbow and eight other whales stayed with Argonaut to winter near Klemtu.

The Inua grew stronger each day. He felt his wound healing. The pain in his side lessened as time passed.

Jason, Matt, General Choate, and the former Coast Guard officers Mendenhall and DeFord visited the Inua almost every day. Argonaut used his power to watch the progress of the pod as they swam west under the watchful eye of Captain Steve Waters and the crew of the USS Independence.

Every day, Argonaut moved his right pectoral fin a little more. He was helping the muscles regain strength. He dove a few feet and quickly resurfaced. He promised to follow instructions. He was a whale true to his word.

In early April, the pod made its way back to Telegraph Cove. Captain Waters and his ship made the journey along with the pod.

Angel and her new calf approached Argonaut.

"Mate, meet your new daughter, Leah Castor. Daughter, meet your father, the great Inua Argonaut," Angel said.

The young whale slowly approached her father and bowed respectfully. With her thoughts said, "Hello great Argonaut. I am happy to meet you. I have heard wonderful stories about you. I am proud to be your daughter."

Argonaut flexed his muscles and the mesh vest that was wrapped around his body snapped. He swam away from the pod and breached again and again.

The entire pod broke out in joyous song. They were glad to see the Inua Argonaut was fully healed. Life was back to normal in the straits of Vancouver Island.

THE END

REGISTERING AS AN ORGAN AND TISSUE DONOR

Approximately 95% of people eligible to register to be organ and tissue donors in the United States say they support registration. However, only about 50% of eligible donors are registered.

Over twenty people a day die in the United States each day waiting for an organ donor match.

The need for additional donors is significant. If you are interested in registering, you can do so online by visiting www.donatelife.net to learn how to register in your home state. You can register when you obtain or renew your driver's license. You can register online at any time.

The gift of life through organ and tissue donations may be the greatest act of human kindness anyone can offer. Do not delay.

Register now, discuss your decision with your family, and make all your end-of-life plans while you are able.

In Canada, there are approximately 4,400 Canadians waiting for a lifesaving organ transplant.

Not everyone in need of a vital organ receives a transplant.

In fact, on average, 250 Canadians die each year waiting for an organ. Public opinion data shows that 90% of Canadians approve of organ and tissue donation yet, only 23% say they have registered their decision to become an organ and tissue donor. With continued investment, support, and collaboration across the country, a world-class organ and tissue donation and transplantation system in Canada is possible.

Every province has its own registry or method for indicating one's intent to donate organs and tissues.

To find out more visit:

https://organtissuedonation.ca/

AUTHOR'S NOTE

The fictional account of the world's first whale organ transplant is based on the author's experiences attending two human organ procurement operations and a heart transplant.

The young directors of Project HOPE address the Canadian Legislature and the general Assembly of the United Nations.

Argonaut is a real whale. The Marine Education Research Society and Orca Lab are actual groups and can be researched online. To learn more about Argonaut and his story please search for THE MARINE DETECTIVE on the internet.

To contact the author, email:
ARGONAUTHUMPBACK@GMAIL.COM